THE
LONELIEST MUSE

Tyger B. Dacosta

iUniverse, LLC.
Bloomington

The Loneliest Muse

Copyright © 2012 Tyger B. Dacosta

iUniverse books may be ordered through booksellers or by contacting:

iUniverse
1663 Liberty Drive
Bloomington, IN 47403
www.iuniverse.com
1-800-Authors (1-800-288-4677)

ISBN: 978-1-4697-9179-1 (sc)
ISBN: 978-1-4697-9181-4 (hc)
ISBN: 978-1-4697-9180-7 (e)

Printed in the United States of America

iUniverse rev. date: 10/28/2013

Contents

Chapter 1

DESTINY'S CHILD

On the Island of Leisha lived the muses, Greek goddesses who existed solely to inspire humankind. Each was gifted to bring their talents to those who needed them most. Clio was the historian gifted with the ability to write all of history, once it had become the past. She did not, however, possess the power of prophecy, as did her sister, Delphi. Clio's job was simply to record events accurately, so that future scholars could learn from them. Signa is the muse of song and dance, inspiring those who dreamed of the performing arts. Calliope is the muse of musicians, Urania of astronomy, the twins Flora and Fauna of horticulture and animal husbandry, Thalia of comedy and tragedy. The youngest of them all was Hope. The rules were simple: one muse, one dream, but no more. The reason for this rule was the fact that there were so many people in the world who needed them, so all should be given a chance.

However, there was one who deserved and needed the muse's help, but for all their powers, they could not help her. It was their little sister, Hope, the loneliest muse. In human terms, Hope looked to be no more than a child of six or seven years of age, but in actuality, she was over two hundred years old, although that is not at all old for a muse. Hope was a wonderful child. She was warm and caring, as well as highly intelligent because of her natural curiosity about the world in which she lived. Even though Hope had her own dilemma, she never became discouraged. She always put aside her own problems in order to help others she felt were more deserving.

You see, Hope had the greatest problem a muse could ever have. Hope lacked the talent to inspire others. Hope excelled in all other aspects: archery, history, music, astronomy, math, plant and animal life, as did all the muses, but each of them specialized in one specific talent. Hope, on the other hand, did not, and although this was troublesome for her, she never let it show. This concerned her sisters so much that, unbeknownst to Hope, they called an emergency meeting. Clio spoke first, as was her right as the eldest.

"As you are all aware, I have called this meeting to discuss how we can help our littlest sister in her hour of need."

"Where is Hope?" Asked Signa.

Clio replied, "Flora asked Hope to gather some special herbs that grow only on the other side of the island, so that we have enough time for discussion." Flora nodded to her sisters.

"Besides," continued Clio, "This matter concerns her personally, as it does us emotionally, and I have asked her to join us when she returns." The muses agreed. "I am certain she will be here soon."

Clio glanced at Delphi, the muse of prophecy, and Delphi spoke.

"As it comes to pass, so shall it be written." Clio was quick to write a note in her tome for future reference.

"Sisters," Clio said, "You are very much aware of the plight our youngest sister Hope faces. She has existed among us for two centuries and has brought great joy to us, her family. Who among you disagrees?"

All in attendance sat silent, as Clio well knew they would. Her statement was just a formality, and she was silently pleased by her sisters' acknowledgement that Hope was indeed loved by them all.

"It saddens me that in all this time, with as many times as she has helped us, she cannot help herself. My heart breaks," continued Clio sadly, "That one as special as she cannot find it within herself to recognize her special talent. Truly, among us all, she is the loneliest muse."

Once again, as was becoming the norm, the muses sat silently helpless. As Clio concluded, all the muses, as if in an orchestrated movement, lowered their eyes to the ground, for they knew Clio spoke the truth.

Fauna, after what seemed an eternity, spoke with a forcefulness not usually seen among them, let alone heard.

"And what of the other gods, what do they have to say about all of this? Or do they choose to sit idly by high on their mountain top? Are we still considered nothing more than an Amazonian petting zoo?" Fauna concluded.

"Sister, please," Clio said, trying to calm Fauna.

She understood the frustration Fauna was feeling, for the male gods had once treated them as such, but that was before the great rebellion, when gods fought gods. Clio shuddered at the remembrance.

Flora spoke.

"Sister, although we are identical in appearance, it is obvious that we are different in thought. Must we run to the other gods to solve our own problems? Are we not goddesses in our own right? We have inspired so many; can we not inspire ourselves for once?"

Fauna looked into her twin sister's eyes and knew she was correct, but what were they to do?

"Maybe," said Fauna, "That is it!" She exclaimed so loudly that she startled those around her. "Clio," Fauna said excitedly, "I assume you have already consulted Delphi in determining Hope's talent?"

"That is correct sister, but I…" Before Clio could conclude her statement, Delphi interrupted her.

"And as I explained to Clio, I cannot see what should be seen, for now I am truly blind."

This statement of Delphi's was utterly remarkable, thought Fauna silently. Though she was physically blind, Delphi could navigate the island by herself and describe everything she saw, or rather did not see, in perfect detail.

"Come out with it," Flora said.

"Yes!" The others chorused eagerly.

"I will tell you," said Fauna. "Or rather Delphi will." She smiled. "Sister, what needs to be done for Hope to find her talent?"

The muses were shocked. They were so certain the answer remained in the past; they completely forgot to ask about the future.

"Ah, the way is clear, but it brings much sadness," replied Delphi.

Signa cried, "You do not mean…?"

"No, dear sisters," Delphi continued, "As is often the case when one inquires about the future, it can be misunderstood. When I spoke of sadness, I spoke the truth, but it is not Hope's sadness; it is ours. In order for Hope to find her destiny, she must do what no other muse has ever done. She must leave our island."

Chapter 2:

THE DECISION

"What?" Asked Calliope quizzically.

"Is this true?" Asked Urania.

"Are you certain?" Asked Signa.

"Sisters, please," said Clio.

Delphi understood her sisters' confusion, for how could they be expected to feel otherwise? They could not understand that, while the future has many paths, there is but one answer. Delphi sighed inwardly and felt it was her duty alone to explain, that which was not the answer they were seeking. Delphi explained that it was indeed true, that she had checked all the timelines possibilities and all led to the same conclusion: Hope must leave the island.

"I am certain," she said sadly, "As certain that the youngest of us now approaches."

Hope was returning from collecting the rare herbs her sister Flora asked her to find. Actually, thought Hope, it was no trouble at all. Yes, these herbs only grew on one part of the island, but Hope so enjoyed helping out when she could and enjoyed exploring on her own. Oh, was that bad of me to have that thought? She asked herself. No, she did not think so. She loved her sisters dearly, but being only two hundred years old, her sisters all believed that it was their duty to mother her, and sometimes she felt they were overprotective. She giggled. For once in her existence she felt truly human, even though that was not the case. Muses are not born like human children. They have no father or mother in that respect; rather, they are created collectively by the thoughts of those who share the same needs.

Sadly, she said aloud, "I wonder who created me? What are they like? Are they even aware of my existence?"

Humans were so silly like that. They did not realize that thoughts and words hold power, in which everyone's dreams create another reality where life has meaning, and harsh words should never be spoken lightly or even at all. Delphi was always telling her,

"Be careful what you wish for; you just might get it."

Hope wished she could find those who created her; they might know her secret talent or whether she even had one at all. At that moment, Hope realized it was getting late and she ran as fast as her tiny legs could carry her. Silly me for daydreaming, she thought, and giggled once more. On the way home, Hope could not help wondering if her sisters suspected the problem she faced. Lately, it seemed normal for one of her sisters to ask each day how she was doing. Hope always answered, "Fine," because she did not want to worry her sisters, when it was more important for them to inspire those who needed them more.

Hope had studied Clio's "Tome of history." Although it was small, it appeared to have endless pages. She had read about all the great people her sisters had inspired. Clio inspired people such as Plato and Socrates; Galileo and Mobius were inspired by Urania. Flora and Fauna helped to inspire genetics by introducing plants and animals to save lives, and Delphi inspired Nostradamus. Each one had a purpose in life that gave her existence meaning. All of her sisters had a special talent except for her, and she could not understand why. As brave as Hope was, it was in rare moments like this when she allowed herself to cry.

"Stop it this instant, young lady!" She said to herself. "You are just being silly. Muses are not born to live our lives; we are born to help others so they can live theirs. We are simply a thought or perhaps a whisper to inspire those who dare to dream."

Hope knew in her heart that, sadly, this was true, for the gods and goddesses of Olympus had decreed this long ago. What good is being a muse, if I lack the talent with which to inspire? This last thought made Hope even sadder. Again, she was beginning to cry, and was wiping her eyes with her tunic when she saw a cocoon on a nearby branch and suddenly realized a small miracle was about to happen. Hope continued to watch in utter amazement as the silken sac began to break apart before her eyes, slowly at first, and then faster, as if that which was inside wanted desperately to be free. In just a moment longer, the once imprisoned creature who fought so hurriedly to be freed from its restraints revealed its wondrous transformation from a caterpillar to a beautiful butterfly.

"Ooh!" Said Hope, as she picked up the butterfly in her hands gently so as not to hurt it. The butterfly was still quite young and was equally as curious about the person it beheld. "No little one, I am not your mother, but I will be your friend."

The young butterfly seemed to ponder this a moment and, sensing no threat from this strange being, climbed to her shoulder and continued to dry itself before it attempted to fly. Hope saw the myriad colors on its wings: red and blue, yellow and orange, green and purple.

"You are a living rainbow!" Hope exclaimed.

The butterfly's maiden flight was wobbly at first, but then the lovely creature became more confident. The butterfly circled her head once as if to thank her and flew away. The miracle of life never ceased to amaze her, and she could not help thinking this was an omen. This minor miracle gave Hope strength in the belief that all living things had a purpose, even a talentless muse. As Hope continued her hurried stride home, she failed to notice a spider inspecting the shell from which the butterfly had just emerged and realizing, had it been there just moments earlier, it would have dined extremely well. For now, though, it had to be satisfied to wait another day.

Hope realized that it was getting late, for the sun was already setting and if she did not arrive on time the other muses would be extremely worried for her safety. She arrived home and was surprised to find no one there to greet her, so she went to her room. As Hope was placing the herbs she had collected for Flora in separate containers, she noticed a note written on parchment in Clio's script. The note said,

"Dear sister, when you are through with your task, please meet us in Nia's observatory. It is extremely important."

"Nia's observatory," said Hope. Nia is the muse of astronomy; although her true name is Urania, it was simpler to call her Nia. The last time Hope and the others went to the observatory, Nia had pointed out a new galaxy being born. Maybe this time, she thought, she would see some falling stars. Hope so enjoyed the way they became brighter and brighter before flickering out. To Hope, it was as if each one was celebrating its own independence in life. Hope arrived and immediately saw her sisters sitting within the open cylindrical columns. Hope hugged each one as she made her way to her seat.

"Sisters," Hope said, "I apologize for being so late. I was enjoying the scenery and was picking these herbs for Flora and lost track of the time. Are these not the finest specimens of plant hood you have ever seen?" Hope passed the vials down to her sister.

Flora stared at the collection of herbs and then lowered her eyes, saying sadly,

"Thank you, Hope; as always you place others' needs before your own."

Hope felt that something was terribly wrong by the way everyone reacted to Flora's statement.

"Is something the matter? Am I in trouble?" Hope asked.

"Child," Clio said, "I am afraid we have some bad news."

"Clio, stop being so melodramatic," said Thalia. "You are scaring her," she scolded.

"I agree," said Nia, the muse of astronomy.

"Forgive me sisters," Clio said, "But as you are all aware, the words are not so easily forthcoming. Hope, although you have chosen to keep silent about your problem, we are family and are quite aware of what troubles you."

"You are?" Asked Hope meekly. "Then you realize I have no special talent," she said mournfully.

"You are very much mistaken," Delphi said adamantly. "Even though your talent is shielded from me, have no misunderstanding as to what the future brings."

Hope suddenly looked into the eyes of her sister of prophecy and for once could see a glimmer of hope as Delphi continued,

"Everything and everyone has a purpose in life, child, although it may not always be so easily understood."

Hope remembered the butterfly moments ago, when she was gathering herbs for Flora.

"What am I to do?" She cried.

"Delphi has foreseen that the only way for you to find your talent, and secure your destiny, is for you to leave the island," Clio stated flatly.

"Leave the island, but why? This is my home," said Hope.

"Gilded walls and marble floors do not a home make," said Clio. "It is the love one shares with others. Remember, little sister; the future is built on the foundations of the past."

"I am sorry, but it is the only way," said Clio.

"When must I leave?" Asked Hope.

"Tomorrow at dawn," Clio replied.

An eerie silence fell, as if the inhabitants of the island knew something monumental was taking place, and its outcome could affect their existence as they knew it. Hope felt restless and could not even think about sleeping. Try as she might, all she could do was look at the constellations in the sky. The cascading waterfall in her room, with its glistening water that reflected the moonlit sky in an iridescent blue, had soothed her so often in her short life, but could not do so tonight. Hope's mind was wandering. In all her life, never had she felt so alone and afraid as she did this night. She knew that, had there truly been another way, her sisters would have found it, but their assurance was still no less comforting. Hope could not help feeling responsible for this problem. Being a child, even an immortal one, she held the childish belief that if she had not been born, things would be better. Unknown to Hope, mortal children also felt at times that this was true. If they were an embarrassment to their family, for instance, they believed that life would be much simpler had they not been born or if, suddenly, they simply ceased to exist. This last thought made Hope more human then she would ever know. The last thought was never expressed by her sisters. Being a child, however, she could only see the negativity of the situation.

"Very well," whispered Hope. "I will leave the island, but know I will always love you and someday if I am able to, I will return." In the next moment, she had fallen fast asleep.

Chapter 3:

BY DAWN'S EARLY LIGHT

As the first rays of dawn peeped over the horizon, Hope awoke to their warmth upon her face. Still not quite awake, Hope wondered whether last night's events were but a terrible dream. She asked herself aloud. "Could it have been brought on by something I ate?" No, that was unlikely, for she had never had a nightmare before. Nightmares were rather shy creatures, related to unicorns and other magical equines, and preferred the comfort of their ilk. Usually, they brought bad dreams to mortals who were deserving of them, as warnings that if they did not change their ways, more were to come. Hope had never encountered one before, because muses were immune to such things, and normally nightmares liked to spend their time in the mortal realm. Humans were always doing something to annoy them. No, it was not a nightmare, because as Hope was wiping the sleep dust from her eyes, she saw in the corner of her room the note Clio had left her.

Hope wished for once that it was a nightmare, but it was not, for just then she heard a gentle knock on her door.

"Hello?" Asked Hope, still tired from having just woken up.

"Good morning, little sister." It was Clio.

"Enter," said Hope.

Standing before her was Clio, whose voice Hope had recognized.

Clio was not quite looking her best. Her hair, normally braided in a Grecian bun, hung loosely down to her shoulders and her golden robes, spun from the finest silk thread, seemed to have taken on an antique brass color. Clio, sensing Hope's scrutiny of her appearance, simply answered that it had been a rough night for everyone.

"I fear," said Clio, "That preparation for today's event has left us all quite disheveled. Your sisters wanted to prepare a going away feast in honor of your journey. I think you will be pleased."

Clio could not bear to look in her youngest sister's eyes and preferred to stare at the marble floor as if a magic spot had just appeared.

Hope, not forgetting her manners, replied,

"I would be most honored, even if it was only breadcrumbs, provided I was sharing it with the ones I love."

"Come then, child, your feast waits," said Clio, as she put an arm around the littlest muse and escorted her proudly to breakfast.

As Clio promised, a fine feast was waiting for Hope. Equally, as Clio had warned, the other muses did not look their best. Exhaustion and sadness could still be seen in their eyes as well as in their actions. Though the finest breads and fruits were laid before them, prepared by her sisters' own hands, no one was less hungry then Hope herself.

Normally, it was a simple matter to prepare for a banquet, as Flora, the muse of horticulture, would simply use the cornucopia. The cornucopia, also called the horn of plenty, was able to produce in abundance whatever food was necessary, but her sisters felt this was a special occasion as well as a sad one and chose to make everything by hand.

Hope thanked her sisters for what they had done, and explained that she had not slept well and preferred to travel on an empty stomach. Her sisters understood as all of the muses simply picked at the food before them. Hope herself settled on a glass of blood orange juice, which was quite rare and tasted delicious. It compared to sparkly wine without the alcohol. Flora had introduced the fruit to humans, but amazingly, very few had ever heard of the wonderful elixir; those who had compared it to ambrosia, the food of the gods. That was silly, Hope thought. No mortal she had ever heard of had tasted ambrosia, but humans were always labeling things.

"Sisters," Clio said finally, "This feast was prepared to honor one among us on the occasion of her journey, and although it saddens us all, the time has come for our sister to depart. Though we have done our best to delay the inevitable, I fear it is time to send the youngest of us on her way."

The muses all sat silent. Each of them wanted to delay this moment, but as is with the present, sooner or later it will become the past. Hope gulped the remains of her juice and sat quietly, as Clio continued to speak.

"Dearest sister, the fates have decreed that you must depart the island of Leisha and, in doing so, you will fulfill your destiny. Though you know it saddens us all, we, your family, cannot stand in your way if we are to hope you will one day return to us. Are you prepared, dear sister?" Clio asked.

"I am," Said Hope bravely.

"Then, sisters, will each of you bring a token of remembrance, to help guide our little sister on her way?"

Hope was not prepared for this, for she thought she was simply to depart without any farewells. Her sisters would not hear of it. Each muse brought a token of their ability to help Hope on her adventure. Nia brought a star map and a telescope to help guide her home. Thalia gave her the gift of laughter to face life's tragedies. Calliope presented her with a lyre to play, and Signa a song of hope. Flora gave her a book on plants, Fauna one on animals. Clio presented a tome in which all of Hope's exploits would be recorded magically, and Delphi gave the greatest gift of all, a chance to fulfill her destiny. Hope thanked each of her sisters, hugged each one as if for the last time, and then they led her down to the shore where a boat waited. She had never seen such a magnificent boat and did not know where it came from. The boat was shaped like a beautiful swan and seemed almost alive.

Clio explained that this boat would take her safely from the island to where she was needed the most but that even though the boat is magical, it had its limits.

"The boat's limited enchantment can take you where you are needed the most and it can bring you home, but the rest is up to you. The pages of your life must be written by your own hand and, whatever the outcome, you must accept responsibility for your actions. Do you understand?"

"Yes," said Hope, but was not sure she did; magic was very funny stuff.

The muses led their little sister down to where the golden swan boat was waiting. Though they all wanted to hug her once more, they fought hard not to do so because they did not want to make Hope's departure any harder than it was already for her and them. Hope fought back the tears that were starting to become obvious to everyone and gently rubbed her eyes dry with the sleeve of her tunic. Resisting the urge to run back to her room and lock the doors so she would not have to leave, Hope did the most grownup thing she had ever done. She turned around, faced forward and, once safely positioned in the boat, directed it to take her where she was needed most. The golden swan boat gave a sign of acknowledgement by honking and started sailing away.

Hope remembered something that Delphi had once told her that made her decision much easier. Delphi had explained that the future, try as one might to delay the

inevitable, will not be prevented from happening, once we let go of the past. Although at the time, Hope did not quite understand the meaning, she could not help but think that Delphi knew that those very words would one day help her in her struggle to make the right decision. Hope looked around for the first time and saw Delphi standing high on the cliff; she was smiling as if she knew what she said so long ago was finally coming true. Hope could not help but smile back. She could hear the beautiful melody being played on one of Calliope's instruments, which was in tune with the words of a song Delphi was singing to her. It was about Hope and the song was even more beautiful as each of the muses joined in chorus. If Hope ever doubted how much she was loved by her sisters, she never doubted it again and promised to whichever gods were listening, that nothing they could do would stop her from returning home.

Chapter 4:

CASTLES IN THE SAND

H ours had come and gone and Hope still had no idea where the beautiful golden swan boat was taking her, but knew it had to be to a place where she was needed, because of the enchantment placed on it. As if responding to her thoughts, the swan boat honked as if to acknowledge this was true and then was silent once more. Hope said to the boat, not knowing if it was truly able to understand her, that she felt tired and wanted to sleep awhile and to let her know when they arrived at their unknown destination.

The swan boat acknowledged her once again by honking, and Hope began to understand that this meant "Yes," at which point she fell fast asleep. Hours passed like days as Hope slept, dreaming about nothing in particular until the swan boat's incessant honking suddenly awakened her.

"What?" Asked Hope wiping the sleep from her eyes. "Where are we?"

Ignoring her question, the boat continued to paddle once it was certain that she was awake. Apparently, thought Hope, this boat takes its duties quite seriously. Hope looked around, not recognizing her surroundings, and asked the swan boat if that was where she needed to be.

The boat honked "Yes."

"I do not understand," Hope said. "We are in the middle of the ocean and far away from home; are you certain you are not mistaken?"

The boat suddenly made short, continuous honks, as if surprised she would even question its reliability. Hope sensed that she had inadvertently offended the boat and apologized quickly. The swan boat gave her a soft honk and she knew it had accepted her apology as it continued to paddle to an unseen destination. Hope still could not see where the boat was taking her and used the telescope her sister Nia had given her. She noticed a rock formation straight ahead of them. As the boat continued to paddle closer to it, the rock formation began to take on a more familiar shape, like that of a house but carved out of rock. Hope noticed that the rock gave off a green, luminescent glow, depending on which way the sun reflected off it. As the swan boat came to rest upon the white shores of the beach, there was no mistaking it: it was indeed a house, and Hope could not help but wonder whose.

She examined the house and realized she had seen this type of rock before; this house had been carved from jade. On the island of Leisha, jade was used for jewelry and other ornate objects due to its strength and beauty. However, this jade was of a rare and unusual type, the kind that only grew underwater. Hope was about to ask the swan boat to leave when she noticed a young girl about fifteen or sixteen years old walking along the beach toward her picking up objects on the ground. Her hair was a golden blond that seemed to flow like the waves lapping at her feet and the coral pink dress she was wearing conformed to her body in all the right places. She was beautiful indeed, thought Hope. Hope disembarked and approached the girl cautiously so as not to frighten her. Once certain that the young girl knew she was not in any danger, Hope walked slowly up the beach toward her.

"Hello, my name is Hope," she said.

"Hello," replied the young girl politely, "My name is Sandy; you are a muse, huh?"

Hope was startled and the perplexed look on her face made the young girl Sandy smile.

"I suppose you are wondering how I knew that," she said.

"Well, yes," replied Hope, still looking confused.

"They told me," she said and pointed toward the ocean.

Hope looked to where Sandy had pointed, but saw no one around. Sandy, seeing Hope's confusion, giggled and replied simply,

"My parents told me."

"Are they on the island too?" Asked Hope.

"Oh no," replied Sandy, "Then they would become beached. My parents prefer to stay far away from the land. See, there they are," said the young girl and pointed once again toward the ocean.

Hope looked around and for the first time noticed a middle-aged couple swimming in the ocean, waving at them. The woman appeared to be an older version of Sandy with one subtle difference: she was topless and well formed. The man was also rather striking, with his muscular build and brown hair and was carrying a rather odd staff with three prongs. Hope waved to Sandy's parents, not understanding why they would swim so far out in the ocean, when the water must be freezing.

"My parents like to scavenge at this time and while they were diving they noticed a strange boat approaching my grotto," she said. "Parents being what they are, they wanted to make sure their only child was not in any danger and so they went to investigate."

"I see," said Hope, still not quite understanding. "But how did they know I was a muse and how can they swim so far out in the ocean?" She asked.

"The first question is easy," Sandy answered, "Your boat told them."

"My boat?" Said Hope, more confused than ever.

"As for your second question, said Sandy, "My parents do not dive as far as they used too. They only dive about two to three hundred feet now. Dad keeps begging mom to go farther, but she says they have to slow down now since they are up in age," Sandy giggled.

Hope replied that in order for them to dive that far they would have to be fish.

"Well," said Sandy slyly, "At least part fish."

"You mean…" asked Hope and before she could finish her sentence, Hope saw Sandy's father standing on his head; instead of feet, he had a tail.

"Dad is always showing off for the ladies," giggled Sandy. "Mom is going to make him pay for that stunt when they get home."

"You are a mermaid?" Asked Hope.

"A mer-girl, to be more precise," replied Sandy.

"I still do not understand how your parents knew that I was a muse" said Hope. "You said my boat told them."

"That is correct," said Sandy, "And as you know, mer-folk are part fish and part human." Most human folk who have encountered us know we can speak in human languages. What most do not realize is that we can also speak in marine languages as well. Technically, your swan boat can only reside in water, thus making it a form of marine life and while you were sleeping, we were able to fathom in great depth the problem you are facing."

Hope at once lowered her eyes; because she knew what Sandy had said was true. She had hoped to keep her secret a while longer from this stranger, because she wanted Sandy to have a chance to get to know her first and not judge her for her misfortunes. Sandy saw that her new friend Hope was starting to get teary-eyed and gently wiped them away with her fingers.

"It is okay," said Sandy, "You have nothing to be ashamed of, because I also have a secret."

"You do?" Asked Hope as she was drying her eyes.

"Oh yes," replied Sandy. "It is what made me an outcast among the mer-folk." Then it was Sandy's turn to get teary-eyed.

"If I may ask," Hope said, as she wiped the salty tears from Sandy's eyes, "What could someone as beautiful as yourself have done to make you feel like an outcast?"

This time the beautiful mer-girl could not hold back her tears, and choked on the words that she had never wanted to repeat to anyone again.

"I am afraid of water!" She sobbed.

Chapter 5:

BEACHED

H ope returned Sandy's favor by wiping away the stream of
tears from her newfound friend's eyes and could not help but
sympathize with Sandy's plight. It must be as devastating
for a mer-girl never to know the ocean as it was for a muse to lack a
talent. Hope was curious as to why this happened to her, but did not
want to put any undue pressure on the mer-girl. Sandy could not contain
the secret anymore, however, and told Hope how night after night she
had wished for somebody, anybody, she could talk to who would be
sympathetic, unlike her fellow mer-folk. Sandy then proceeded to tell
Hope her story as the muse sat listening to her patiently.

Sandy told her,

"It happened about fifteen years ago when I was born. My father
and mother were so overjoyed to give birth to their first mer-baby that
they scoured the sea for trinkets with which to decorate the grotto. In
his youth, my father discovered a cave that grew the most beautiful
underwater jade ever seen. He kept this secret to himself, hoping one
day to find the perfect mate and build her the most beautiful grotto. A
few years later he met my mother and they both fell in love and married.
He kept his mer-boy promise and proceeded to carve out a home for
him and my mother. A year later I was born. Mom and Dad were so

proud of their mer-baby that they decided to name me Sandy. They felt so overwhelmed by the joy I brought them, that each day they would scour the sea for fresh kelp for my sea bed. We were very happy," Sandy said. "That is, until fate decided to tear our family apart forever," she cried.

Hope was intrigued by Sandy's story and asked her what had happened.

"The great sea-quake." She replied, shuddering. "Mer-folk were always running into storms and we would avoid them simply by diving deep below the water, but a sea-quake is harder to avoid," she said. "My parents had left the grotto to go on their usual scavenger hunt for food and kelp and had just dived a hundred meters when the quake struck. I started to cry because I was scared as my parents tried to swim back to where I was but the sea-quake, which had created serious riptides, stirred the ocean's floor with such fury that the sands blinded them and they were helpless to comfort their mer-baby's cries for help. As I lay clutching to whatever I could for comfort, the grotto started to rise higher and higher as the surroundings came crashing down upon me," she said. "My parents grasped at the ocean floor, trying desperately to reach me, but to no avail. They watched in terror as their only child was being taken away from them, feeling guilt for not doing something more for their mer-baby. That is how I ended up beached on this island and why I am so afraid of water," she said sadly.

"My parents sent the local marine life to check up on me, and would show the sea-gulls for example, where they could find an abundance of krill in exchange for feeding me. Once they had their fill, they would chew up the rest in small bites and feed me as a mama bird does her chicks. Then, one day, a mother sea-lion came ashore to nurse her pups, and hearing a strange sound, went to investigate. She saw that I was alone and hungry and assumed I had been abandoned. Her maternal instincts took over and she pushed this strange creature with her nose to where her pups were lying in wait and allowed me to nurse. The pups at first seemed to resent such a strange creature, but after their mother barked at them, they learned to accept me. Finally, the mother sea-lion needed to return to the sea with her pups, because they were older and capable of swimming on their own. One by one the pups slid into the water, but when it was my turn to go, I refused to budge. Trying as any mother would to get her reluctant child to do what she wanted, the mother sea-lion pushed me with her nose, but I cried every time I came near the water. She barked at me and pushed me once again with her nose and body, but I would not go in and made my way back to the beach. Having given up to my stubbornness, the mother sea-lion made one last plea as she dove into the water. Sensing the fear and apprehension of her adopted child, she looked back as if to say, 'Take care,' and I never saw her again."

Hope started to cry as Sandy concluded her story; she knew what her friend was feeling, for she felt it too. Hope could understand what it was like to be different and did not want anybody else to go through what she had. She asked Sandy,

"Would you like to join me on my adventure?"

Sandy agreed readily and told Hope she wanted to retrieve some items from her grotto, such as a sea sponge, coral comb and some food for them, and went to her grotto in order to get them. Moments later Sandy returned with the items. Upon seeing the swan boat, Sandy had reservations about it being sea-worthy. Hope assured her that it was and so Sandy climbed in and positioned herself safely in the middle of the boat. Hope asked the swan boat if it was alright to bring her, the boat honked in assent, and off they went. As they sailed farther away from the island, Sandy's parents swam alongside the boat, guiding it safely away from unseen rock formations. Sandy and Hope waved to them both as they sailed off into the sunset.

Chapter 6:

A WING AND A PRAYER

Iggi was tired and irritable, as usual, which was brought on by hunger as well as exhaustion from fighting with his wings. The stale piece of bread left over from last night's meal nearly broke his tooth, as well as the wall at which he threw it in frustration. He knew he would have to leave his cave in search of those strange but wondrous mushrooms he had found so long ago. The fairy mushrooms he had discovered only grew in a damp part of the forest near the cave he had found and only lasted a few hours each day in the hot sun. As the early morning sun rose higher and higher and the day became hotter, the mushrooms shriveled up and were no good to eat. Thus, he knew that if he wanted to satisfy this growing hunger, he would have to make a decision quickly, as already he could feel the heat of the day on his face and his hunger pangs were growing loud. He was certain that, had the other fairies known where the mushrooms grew, they would have been picked already.

The reason he was having trouble deciding what to do was because of his blasted wings. It was one thing for the fairies to comment on his unusual size, being four-feet tall, but it was another thing for them to see him arguing with his wings and losing. It was bad enough being a freak, but even worse when your wings were the size of a normal fairy's and seemed to have a mind of their own. As Iggi grew, his wings remained small and could not support his weight when he tried to fly; thus, he remained grounded.

The other fairies would flutter about him and ask him teasingly to come join them, knowing he could not. One day Iggi decided enough was enough and the next time they flew around him, he broke off the nearest branch and swatted at them like flies. Fairies were falling left and right on the ground and as Iggi made sure they were alright, he apologized for losing his temper and told them it would not happen again. The fairies were uncertain of his sincerity because of the gleam in his eyes and decided it was best not to tease him like that again. Iggi grumbled to himself that he was fed up and stormed off to his tree. Once there, he threw everything he could fit haphazardly into his knapsack. The exception to that was his best friend, a little rag doll named Tuff, which he placed gently in the top of his knapsack. Iggi normally did not refer to Tuff as a doll because he felt he was so much more. Tuff was shaped like a little man and was nothing more than pieces of string and straw held together by bees' wax and clay.

As a child, Iggi always felt different from the others and his size did not help matters. Lonely and confused by his strange appearance, he wished for a friend, one who would listen to him and not judge him for his differences. Sure, the other fairy children had imaginary friends, but Iggi craved something more special. He had mixed water with mud and created clay but, try as he might, his little friend kept falling apart. And, try as he might, he could not seem to find a way to keep his little friend together; time after time, the results were the same. Frustrated, Iggi would lie down beneath his tree and stare at the clouds for hours.

Then something struck him, quite literally, on the head. He remembered he was looking up at his tree when a passing bird flew by carrying bits of string and acorns with which to build a nest; it dropped one on his head. Every day, as Iggi sat watching the bird, it carried pieces of twine, plants and whatever else it could find to build its nest. After a few days, the bird had gathered enough odds and ends and proceeded to build its nest. It had also found an abandoned hive with remnants of honey and would dip its beak in one side and then another, after which it would fly back to its nest, repeating the same steps inside and out.

After a few days, Iggi was amazed to see how all the pieces stuck together. He was impressed by the bird's ingenuity and wondered if the same could be done for Tuff. Many days later, and after many attempts, Tuff was born. Iggi was tired of living in a tree because he had found that it was not as comfortable for oversized fairies as it was for birds. So Iggi set off to find a new home for himself and his best friend. He eventually came upon an abandoned cave and moved in after he made certain that nothing else was going to climb in bed with him unexpectedly. Iggi made this cave look remarkably like a home and was pleased with his interior decorations. A few days later, Iggi heard the other fairies whispering to each other as he walked past them.

"He is a menace," said one.

"I agree," said another.

"He is going to eat us out of house and home," said a rather over-healthy one as he gobbled on four sandwiches.

Gathered by the oleander bush, the fairies were too busy complaining about Iggi, for had they looked up at that moment they would have noticed him sneaking up on them.

"Boo!" Yelled Iggi, as each of the fairies fell to the ground shuddering uncontrollably, as if an invisible giant's hand had splattered them on the ground.

"Hmm," said Iggi, sounding proud, "That'll teach you!" There's nothing worse than a bunch of gossiping fairies," he grumbled as he made his way back to the cave.

Iggi could not resist looking back at them as they continued to shudder on the ground. He soon arrived back at his cave and was still hungry, which was obvious from the way he kept slamming things around the cave. Iggi was always most irritable when he was hungry. He opened a cupboard and found another piece of stale bread left over from last night's dinner. Iggi popped it into his mouth and nearly broke another tooth on the rock-hard piece of bread. Iggi threw that stale piece of bread at the wall as well and as he turned around, it bounced off and hit him in the head.

"Ouch," he said as he felt a welt form where the piece of bread hit him. "Serves me right," he grumbled. "Now I have to go back outside and freeze my wings off, if I don't want to starve to death."

Iggi knew that if he wanted to eat today then he had no choice but to brave the cold morning; he would try to pick as many mushrooms as possible to avoid having to repeat the task tomorrow. Already the cave was starting to warm up, telling him he had better go now before it was too late. As Iggi opened the door to his cave, he felt the cool air rushing in to meet him. "Brrr," he said, as goose-bumps appeared on his arms; Iggi hated the length of time it took to de-ice his wings, but hated the idea of starving even worse. As he felt the cold wind seeping into his wings, Iggi ran as fast as his legs could carry him to where his secret stash of mushrooms grew. Thankfully, when Iggi arrived at his secret garden, the mushrooms were undisturbed. Fortunately for him, no one yet knew about them. Even more fortunately, they grew in abundance if anyone ever did discover them. Iggi knew he could pick the lot of them without any worry because, unlike the others, they always grew back the next day. Iggi had grabbed the knapsack in which to put the handful of mushrooms he was carrying when his wings started to flutter suddenly, which irritated the heck out of him.

"Stop that," he grumbled, but the tiny wings refused to obey him, as if they were trying to shake off the cold themselves. Iggi reached around to swat at his wings as they continued to flutter. The effort caused him to twist and turn in all directions. The fairy folk had seen this many times and found it quite amusing, but to Iggi it was a real nuisance. As Iggi tossed and turned trying to swat at his wings, he failed to see a rock at his feet and went tumbling down the hill, where he landed in a patch of thorn-berries.

"Ouch," he said as he pulled them from the seat of his pants. "See what you made me do?"

He was about to let out a not so fairy-like word as he got up and dusted himself off when he saw a strange-looking boat about to dock. Iggi peered out from the bush so as not to be seen and noticed two girls getting off the boat. The taller girl was helping the smaller one get off the boat and as each one stepped onto the beach, they looked around as if searching for someone or something. Iggi knew every inch of this island and knew very well that there was no treasure to be found. On occasion he would find some shells or maybe some driftwood but those things were common on any beach. So, if it was not treasure they were looking for, then it had to be a person but who, he wondered? Iggi was not the brightest of the fairy-folk, but if they meant to cause harm to one of his own, no matter how annoying they might be, they were in for a big surprise. Iggi did not condone violence, but felt that as a misfit, his life was insignificant and he had to do what he could to protect the fairy-folk; then, maybe they might remember him as a hero. Iggi took a deep breath. He knew what he had to do, so he mustered all his courage, and marched toward the two strangers. Iggi did not realize that because of that simple act of bravery, his life was about to change drastically.

Chapter 7:

WINGING IT

Iggi could not help but stare at the two strangers who were now fast approaching him. One looked to be about six years old, with a dark complexion and wearing some kind of tunic; her hair was curled in a pony-tail. The other, the taller of the two, looked to be about fifteen years of age. She had golden hair and wore a long dress that seemed to shimmer like the waves lapping at her feet. They did not look dangerous, but Iggi did not like strangers on his island and he was going to make sure they left immediately. Iggi stood his ground, watching ever so closely as the two girls approached his hiding place. He noticed that they seemed to be looking for something or perhaps someone, but he was the only one who resided on this part of the island and he had never seen these two before in his life. Why are they here? He wondered. Nevertheless, Iggi did not want them here for whatever reason, and he was going to rectify that at once.

"Get off my island!" He shouted, still hidden from view of the two strangers. "You're trespassing. Leave at once!"

This startled the two girls, for as they looked around they could see no one.

"Who are you?" Asked the smaller of the two.

"Show yourself at once!" Demanded the taller girl. "It is rude to yell at people when they cannot see you."

Iggi could not help but smile at the taller girl's boldness, but he was not the type to be bullied by the likes of her. What if they discovered his terrible disability? No, even if these strangers meant him no harm, he could not risk them discovering his secret.

"I said, get off my island. You're not welcome here!" Iggi yelled as he stormed out of the bushes where the two girls could see him.

This set off the taller of the two girls, who approached Iggi boldly while the smaller of the two was more cautious.

"Listen here," she said. "We have come a long way and we are both tired and hungry and some demented *elf* with an attitude is not going to stop us from finding what we need."

With the last statement, she stared face to face with Iggi, her hands on her waist. Iggi knew she meant what she said, just as sure as he was that they were not going to leave until they found what they wanted. Iggi could not help but wonder what it was, exactly, that they were looking for on the island. Iggi had lived here all of his life and was certain there was nothing of value. He knew every square inch of the island. Oh, occasionally some unusual sea-shell from some creature of long ago washed up, but nothing of true value. Maybe they were not exactly telling him the truth. Maybe they were really after something else: but what was it? Iggi had no idea, but he was sure going to find out.

"I'm not an *elf*. I'm a fairy."

The girls' faces dropped as they eyed Iggi up and down; then they looked at each other and started to laugh.

"What're you laughing at?" Iggi demanded to know.

"That is funny," said the taller of the two.

"What are you really?" Inquired the smaller one.

"I told you I'm a fairy!" Iggi started to stamp his feet and throw a tantrum, forgetting all about what happened when he lost control.

In the next instant, Iggi's wings, which were normally hidden by his enormous size, started to beat rapidly as if to say 'We are here!'

The girls looked astonished once again, as they actually noticed for the first time that the strange little elf did indeed have wings, tiny as they were.

"Hey, that is cute," said the smaller girl.

"Do that again," said the taller of the two.

"I will not!" Said Iggi gruffly and walked away, mumbling. The last thing they saw was him shaking his head and saying "Girls!"

The two could hear the funny little fellow grumbling as he continued to walk away. At first they thought he was talking to them but then realized that he was actually talking to his wings. The wings continued to flutter uncontrollably like a misbehaving child, but like all children, soon grew tired of the game and stopped. The girls sensed the frustration and embarrassment he was feeling, for they too understood what it was like to be different. The girls followed him and quickly introduced themselves while their newfound acquaintance stopped, faced them and lowered his eyes, as if waiting for the inevitable laughter he had faced so many times. Instead, he was surprised to hear understanding in their voices. Iggi learned from them that the smaller of the two girls, who looked to be the youngest, was actually a muse over two hundred years old. He listened with great interest as she relayed the tale of her dilemma and what her sister Delphi, the muse of prophecy, told her and how the strange boat, which was magically sentient, could help her and those like her. Then it was the taller of the two girl's turn. He found out that she was a mer-girl named Sandy. Sandy related an equally sad tale about being separated from her folk and her unnatural fear of water. Iggi was dumbfounded that these two strangers, who were themselves facing equally devastating problems in their lives, could actually put aside their own troubles and want to help him.

The girls were just as curious to find out about Iggi who, with some reluctance, explained his problem. As Iggi sensed, the girls did seem concerned and wanted to help him if they could. They excused themselves for a few moments and walked over to where the beautiful swan boat that carried them to the island lay and seemed to converse with it. Iggi noticed the way the unusual boat craned its neck as if it was listening carefully to what the girls were saying and then replied with a resounding honk. The girls seemed to share a common joy as they quickly explained it was him that they were searching for and that the swan boat's honk was a sound of approval.

Iggi did not fully understand, for his talent of comprehension was almost nil, so the girls explained as best they could. As foreseen by Hope's sister Delphi, the boat could only take her to where she was needed most. It did not necessarily mean to a *place* of importance, but to a *person* of importance, and the boat agreed that it was Iggi for whom they were actually searching. Iggi could not believe what they were saying, that somebody actually thought *he* was important. Iggi's' mind began to flood with all sorts of questions. Why would someone consider a four-foot fairy with tiny wings important to the girl's mission and how could they help him solve his own problem? Iggi could not figure it out, but he had to admit he was starting to like the two girls and if he could, he would help them.

"First things first," he said. "I know a safe place where you can rest for the night and get something to eat."

The girls were overjoyed, for the trip had been long and arduous and anywhere was better than sleeping on the boat.

"Okay," Hope and Sandy said in unison and followed Iggi along the path where they had first encountered him. The girls knew better than to trust a stranger they had just met, but they were cold and tired and the magical boat had been instructed to bring them to where they were needed most. Hope was certain they were in no immediate danger from their newfound friend but told Sandy they should be careful nonetheless. Sandy agreed and told Hope that if either of them felt the least bit threatened they would leave immediately, but moments before they were out of sight, the boat, sensing their unheard thoughts, gave them a reassuring honk to say they were safe. After a few minutes, the girls came to a cave entrance. Iggi rushed inside and Hope and Sandy followed; at first it was dark and they could not see where Iggi was, but soon they heard him rustling ahead.

"Just a minute," he said. "Stay where you are!"

In the next few moments, as the girls stood in the dark corridor, a green glow started to fill up the cave and the girls were able to see the enormous space that loomed before them. Obviously, Hope thought silently, an oversized fairy would need a big cave. Sandy, too, was amazed at the size and seemed to be sad.

"What is wrong?" Asked Hope.

"I was just thinking about home and how much this place reminds me of my own grotto."

Hope understood; she too missed home, but at least this place was big enough for the three of them. Hope gave Sandy a hug as a way of saying they would be home again soon. Sandy appreciated the sentiment and followed Iggi's voice deeper into the cave. Iggi was scrambling around fast, mumbling out loud that he was not expecting guests, which was apparent by the clothes scattered on the floor. Iggi ran around the cave, busily shoving things in drawers when Sandy noticed a strange little doll sitting on the shelf. It seemed to be made of tattered cloth and string and some kind of wax and resembled a little person. Sandy was about to pick it up, when Iggi noticed her and quickly snatched it out of her hand.

"Leave him alone!" Snapped Iggi.

Again, the girls were startled by Iggi's sudden outburst, which had torn the little doll nearly in half.

"I am sorry," said Sandy, "I was just admiring him."

Iggi was sorry too and explained to the girls the importance of his little friend. Iggi had named the little scrap of a person Tuff, he said, and found him to be the best friend he ever had. Tuff never judged him and sat listening patiently to him whenever he was worried or scared or felt alone. The girls seemed to understand his need for a friend, for how many times had they wished they could find someone who would truly understand them. Sandy apologized to Iggi again and he surprised them in return by allowing them to hold the little rag doll.

Sandy was the first and noticed how life-like and detailed he seemed to be, even if he was made of odds and ends. Then Sandy handed the little figure gently to Hope, who was as amazed as was Sandy at the life-like qualities he had. Hope also thought she felt something even more amazing, a beat almost like that of a human heart, but she was sure she was mistaken. She was tired and the mind liked to play tricks on a person in that condition; still, she was uncertain what it was she actually felt. Sandy noticed the startled look on Hope's face in that brief instant, but when she looked at her again, saw that Hope was back to normal. Sandy was concerned for her friend, but dismissed it as fatigue, something she was feeling equally. Iggi had finally finished cleaning the cave and went to the kitchen immediately and started cooking. In a few moments he brought them each a bowl of mushroom soup, which the girls devoured ravenously. He then apologized to them about the lack of rooms, but assured them that they would be quite comfortable in his room. After a few moments of polite declination, he was able to talk them into accepting his offer. Iggi assured them that he was too excited to sleep anyway and wanted to make sure that his items were packed by morning. Hope told him it was best if they left by dawn because they were uncertain of the length of time it would take to get to their next destination. Iggi saw that both of the girls were yawning and he bade them a good night's rest as the girls retreated into his room. Hope had told him that they did not know where they would go next but to pack as much as he was able to carry.

Iggi stayed up the rest of the night, gathering those items he thought might be useful to their quest, clothes and, most importantly, enough food to sustain the three of them. All the while, Tuff sat there on the shelf, observing his long-time friend patiently, and when Iggi looked up at him the rag doll seemed a little sad.

"Don't worry," Iggi said to him, "I would never leave my best friend behind." The little rag doll seemed to brighten up at hearing these words. Dawn came quicker than even Iggi remembered and the girls could be heard rustling around the room. Just as Iggi was placing Tuff in his bag, the door to the room opened and the two girls entered, looking much more refreshed then they had the previous night.

"Good morning," said Hope.

"What time is it?" Asked Sandy rather sleepily.

"Time to start our next day's adventure," said Hope. "Come on, sleepyhead, wake up."

"Anyway," said Sandy as she smiled at Hope. "Youth is wasted on the young."

This time it was Hope who smiled back at her and said, "You forget I am over two hundred years old."

Iggi looked at the two girls, who in return looked at him, and all at once they started to laugh. Iggi could not remember the last time he felt this good, but he hoped he would be able to feel like this again. Iggi offered the two girls' breakfast, but they said they were not really hungry. Hope explained to Iggi again that Delphi was unable to guarantee success, but had told her that this was her only chance. Hope then showed Iggi the magical tome that recorded all the events up to where they were now. Iggi read the book and Hope was correct about the great detail it provided up to the moment that he read it. He could not believe how accurate it was and that it even recorded him reading the book, as words appeared instantly. From his understanding, Clio, the muse of history, had told her little sister that it was up to them how the future was to be written, that once it became the past, only then could the words be recorded. Great, thought Iggi, a muse with a sense of humor. Iggi liked books but always skipped ahead to save time; maybe there was a way around this book.

"Book," he ordered, "Show me the history of Hope."

The book lit up with a glow and showed in great detail all that had transpired with Hope and the heartbreak of her dilemma. Then he asked the book to show him Sandy's history and, once again, he was shown the accuracy of all that had transpired. Hmm, thought Iggi, maybe it can show us the history of those we will meet next. He thought if the book only showed that which had already happened, they might be able to get a jump on what was to happen next.

"Book," he said aloud, "Show us the history of who we'll meet next."

The book just sat there unmoving, unlike the moment before, and was blank.

"Look, you stupid book," he said rather irritably, "You can only show us what has happened already and I get that, but what happened to those next already happened to them, so why can't you show us?"

As Iggi grew more impatient, his tiny wings started to flutter and buzz rapidly.

"Not you too?" He grumbled. The book, being inanimate, did not care what he was feeling; his request was a technicality and magic was more specific, so it did not respond.

"Oh forget it!" He said, "And as for you…" Iggi started swatting at his wings, which in turn caused him to spin around while the two girls watched in amusement.

"Enough of the floor-show," said Sandy. "If you are through we need to get ready."

Iggi grumbled under his breath, "Girls!"

Sandy, who overheard the funny little fairy, looked at Hope in turn and said, "Boys!" Iggi was finally done packing as the new day was beginning, not so much due to his excitement, which was obvious, but to the girl's insistence on helping him.

"Are we ready?" Asked Sandy, looking rather impatient.

"Just a sec, fish-breath, I want to take one last look." Iggi glanced around at the cave he had called home for so long. He remembered that it felt much bigger, but now seemed small to him and plain. Iggi sighed to himself and to no one and the girls understood once again. They remembered a time when the feeling of being part of a magical world meant something, but knowing that a small part of you was missing, seemed to clarify the illusion and the magic faded away. Iggi made sure that Tuff was comfortable peeking out of Iggi's knap-sack and closed the door to his past, hoping silently in his heart, that maybe, once again, he could believe in a happy ending. Iggi walked hurriedly, passing the girls to lead the way, but it was just a short distance to where they had left the beautiful swan boat. When they arrived, they found it waiting for them patiently. The girls hugged the boat excitedly, which in turn gave them a honk as if it was glad to see them.

"That's weird," said Iggi out loud, not meaning to be heard.

"What is so weird about it?" Asked Hope.

"Yes, do tell, small-fry," said Sandy.

"Well, talking to the boat as if it was alive, if you really want to know fish-out-of-water and muse-less."

This time it was Hope who turned to Iggi and asked,

"Any more weird than talking to Fluff the doll?"

This even made Sandy look, astonished at what Hope said, but obviously having had an influence on her friend.

"Yeah, what she said," replied Sandy smartly.

This irked Iggi so much that his wings flapped wildly.

"His name's not Fluff. It's Tuff and he's as real as that boat of yours and, as for you…" Once again Iggi was swirling and twirling and swatting at his wings, which seemed to have their own free will.

Sandy was about to reply once again but was stopped by the boat's rapid honking, as if it was irritated by their banter. This snapped the three adventurers back to reality and, as they looked at each other, they started to laugh once again.

"Great!" Iggi chuckled. "What a three-some we make: a four-foot fairy, a beached mer-girl and a talentless-muse. Whoever reads about our little adventure is going to laugh themselves silly."

After a few more moments of their giggling, the boat seemed most anxious to leave the island, for it sensed more of these times to come. Iggi was the last to get on the unusual craft, wondering aloud if it could even support the three of them, but Hope assured him that the magic kept them safe as long as they were on it; still, Iggi was not so certain. Only when the boat sailed gently on the waves did he feel more secure. Hope explained all she knew about the boats magical animation and the charm it provided them but, thought Iggi silently, what if it was not enough, what would they do then? Even as Iggi worried about their uncertain fate, the boat sailed gently away and the island they had just departed became smaller and smaller until it faded in the distance. By the rising sun's position, hours had come and gone since their departure.

Hope was certain it had been about two hours, for Nia the muse of astronomy had taught Hope her lessons well. Hope remembered how Nia gave her extra lessons in navigation by the stars. Hope only remembered once asking her why she needed to learn navigation, when all the muses stayed on the island.

Nia answered, "Because, dear sister, it is always best to be prepared for the unknown, rather than to be taken by surprise."

Hope accepted this, as was her nature, and never questioned her lessons again. Iggi looked around at the seascape, just an endless ocean; he was very excited once he got used to the adjustments the boat made as it paddled its way to their unknown destination. Wave after wave came but the boat just ignored them as it compensated for the endless surges. Iggi looked at the others and saw that Hope was reading the tome as words suddenly appeared, hoping for some hint of what was to come, but Sandy seemed apprehensive, as if the sea itself was targeting her, making her fear that which was a natural part of herself. Iggi noticed also that she seemed to have a greenish tint to her otherwise amber skin, which adapted her to fit in more readily to her adopted home.

Iggi was still unaccustomed to the politeness necessary in dealing with people, having been isolated for so long. He tried to say something clever, and inadvertently asked Sandy if she wanted to see the flying fish performing what seemed to be impossible feats of flying with acrobatic precision.

Sandy's reply was a simple "No" but inside, she envied them for their comfort in the water. She could not look but a moment at their feats of wonder, for the fear inside her became overwhelming. Hope looked up for just a moment at Sandy's seal-like eyes, almost pleading for her inner strength to take charge, telling her they would always be there and she would never be truly alone. Sandy liked Hope, especially the uncanny way she knew what to say in every situation. She felt at ease with her and even the demented fairy was starting to grow on her, once she ignored his over-sensitivity to his situation.

Sandy did not like to critique others' defects, especially as she herself had one, but she could not help smile at the way Iggi's wings would not give up trying to fly. It had happened their first night together, when they went to bed in the cave. Hope was extremely tired and fell fast asleep, but Sandy could not sleep, try as she might, and after an hour of fighting it got up to see if Iggi needed help packing. What she saw made her smile; Iggi was standing on a chair having a discussion with his wings. It was as if he was purposely trying to antagonize them into some miraculous feat. He was arguing with them and calling them names, saying he wished they would just wither away. This indeed seemed to agitate them into a frenzy and with a leap of faith, Iggi jumped and fell on the floor. He did this numerous times, each time with the same result. He finally gave up and grumbled something incomprehensible. Sandy did not want to embarrass him further, even though this little troll-boy was getting on her nerves, so she closed the door quietly and went back to bed. Hope was still sound asleep and so Sandy closed her eyes and eventually was able to sleep.

Chapter 8:

HORSE SENSE

T he next morning, Sandy was startled suddenly from her thoughts by the honking of the swan boat. She and the others looked where the boat was headed and noticed another island fast approaching them. The others were equally anxious as the unending vastness of the sea was finally wearing them down. Hope clung to the tome as Iggi hung onto the swan boat's neck, hoping to see exactly where the boat was heading. As the tiny island expanded in size as they approached it, Sandy noticed that, unlike Iggi's and her islands, this one was a veritable forest with dense brush and rolling hills, a virtual paradise. Hope also thought to herself how much like home it seemed with its natural beauty and could not wait to find what or, as they discovered, who it was they were looking for in this untamed wilderness.

Iggi was the first to set foot on land, even after the girls warned him of the possible dangers.

"Forget it!" He said as he jumped off the boat. "I've been stuck on this boat way too long and I need to stretch my legs."

The girls indeed noticed that his legs seemed rubbery as he adjusted to the land. Hope and Sandy also had trouble walking but as they held on to each other for support, they seemed to get re-acclimated much more easily than Iggi.

"See, what did I tell you; there's no one here and if there's no one…"

Just as Iggi was about to finish his sentence, an arrow came soaring out of the forest from nowhere and nearly pegged the fairy. "Ahh, he said, "Someone is trying to kill me," and he ran as fast as his legs could carry him back to the comfort of the boat. Hope and Sandy were indeed shocked at this unwarranted attack; they had only come to this island hoping to find what they needed, but if whoever this was who exhibited such hostility toward strangers did not want them here, then they would be most happy to leave.

"We have to find out who it was who attacked us," said Sandy, not believing her own words.

"I know," said Hope, "But maybe it would be best not to anger whoever it is any more than we already have done."

Iggi was sitting in the boat, shaking. For all his bravado, he was as afraid as the rest of them. While Sandy was as scared as he was, she thought something had to be done. Hope asked the boat if they were in danger, but the boat honked a resounding "No." If the boat was correct in saying they were in no danger, why then was someone shooting at them? Hope's mind was full of questions and she could think of no answers. Could this be some sort of twisted test they needed to pass? Whatever the reason, she was certain the answer lay in wait for them past the glade of trees that were blocking their view.

Hope told them her idea that, in order for them to find the truth, they would need to risk leaving the safety of the boat to find the person responsible. Iggi refused and insisted they stay safely put. He was soon out-voted by the other two. Sandy pointed out that the answer to what they were seeking might lie beyond the forest. Iggi knew that arguing with women's logic was next to impossible, so he soon gave in to them. Hope wanted to go first, but Iggi volunteered to lead them. For whatever reason, he felt that somehow he would end up in that position anyhow. As the girls followed him, looking around carefully for danger, Iggi bravely trekked forward with Tuff in tow in his knapsack. As they moved deeper into the vast forest of trees, Iggi thought that they were being attacked by their unknown assailant once again, and took cover quickly, leaving the girls to fend for themselves. It was Sandy who realized that they were not being attacked at all, but that squirrels had been dropping nuts as they leapt from tree to tree. The girls laughed once again, which was becoming a common occurrence, while Iggi picked up a rock and threw it at the trees above them.

"Stupid rodents!" He shouted at the trees, shaking his fist.

"Never mind the squirrels," said Sandy. "We have bigger trouble ahead."

Iggi and Hope looked to where the mer-girl was pointing and saw that what she said was true. Partially hidden in the brush was a man with a bow and arrow, and he was once again taking aim in their direction.

"That is no man," said Sandy, "But a boy. What kind of parents would let their child play with such a dangerous weapon?"

"We can worry about that later," said Hope. "The problem is how we avoid getting shot. Certainly we can avoid one, but he is carrying more on his back."

Iggi too noticed that this boy did indeed have more arrows in a quiver attached by a leather strap across his bare chest.

"What're we going to do?" Asked Iggi nervously as he hung on to Tuff tightly.

"Maybe we can distract him long enough to disarm him," said Sandy. Hope was wishing for some sort of guidance but was as perplexed as the others about what to do.

"Give me your doll," said Sandy. "I think I have an idea."

"What? Are you crazy, barnacle-girl? There's no way I'm going to let you hurt Tuff." In his agitation his wings began to flap rapidly.

"What is your idea?" Asked Hope.

"I am thinking," Sandy said methodically, "That if we can get Tuff near the boy and toss a rock in his direction, we can get him before he gets us."

"You are not going to harm him, are you?" Asked Hope.

"No, of course not, but we need to cause a distraction to attract his attention. Then maybe we can ask him why he is trying to harm us."

Hope nodded; it was not the best plan, but it was the only one they had.

"Wait just a minute," said Iggi. "You want me to risk my best friend's life on a plan that may not even work? You've got algae for brains, tuna-breath."

"Listen," said Sandy anxiously, "I do not like this plan any more than you, but Tuff is the only one who can survive an arrow. We, on the other hand, cannot."

Iggi knew this was true because Tuff was made of wax and string; still, he did not like risking his best friend's life.

"Please," said Hope, "It is our only chance."

Iggi thought long and hard and seemed to confer with Tuff and, strangely enough, Iggi agreed, however reluctantly.

"Fine, but if anything happens to him, I'm going to have the biggest fish-fry ever seen."

Sandy shuddered at his words even though she knew he was joking, or so she hoped, and reached for the little rag doll.

"Forget it!" Iggi said, and this time his wings agreed by their uncontrollable flapping. "If anyone's going to do it, it's going to be me."

How brave the fairy with an attitude was becoming; maybe he has some good in him, Sandy thought silently. Iggi snuck up carefully to where the boy was, still half hidden in the brush. Iggi placed his friend on a branch of a bush and stayed close by, silent. As she picked up a rock to throw, Hope told Sandy Iggi was in position.

Sandy could see that the boy was ready to fire another arrow and told Hope,

"Now!"

Hope threw the rock toward Tuff, barely missing Iggi, who was probably fuming. The boy looked at the place where he heard the sound.

"What are you?" Asked the boy, pointing the arrow downwards as he reached for Tuff.

Just then Iggi leapt from his hiding place and jumped on the boy's back, shouting,

"I got you now!" But, as he leapt on what he thought was the boy's back, he was shocked to find a horse body instead.

"Get off me!" Shouted the horse-boy, kicking out with his forefeet and bucking wildly.

Sandy and Hope noticed immediately what the brush had hidden from view; this was no boy at all. He was, in fact, a centaur. Hope had read all about the centaurs in her history class. They originated from a love spring where a human and horse had fallen in love. They produced an offspring, which had characteristics of both. Centuries later, they had created a herd and eventually sought out privacy. No one knew exactly where they had disappeared, but now Hope and her friends had discovered that they must have migrated somehow to this island. Iggi, too, had discovered his mistake a little too late and was now riding someone who did not want to be ridden.

"Get off me," yelled the centaur-boy again, still bucking and kicking frantically, trying desperately to get off this most unwelcome intruder.

"I'm trying," Iggi said breathlessly, "But you need to calm down!"

The centaur did not hear his reply, as he thrust his hind end high up in the air with all his might and threw Iggi into a nearby bush.

"Owww," Iggi said, rubbing his rear. "You're going to pay for that."

The girls rushed to where their friend was lying in the bush and tried to lift him to his feet.

"That was some ride," Iggi said dizzily.

"Are you alright?" Asked Hope.

"He looks okay, but I think his ego will take some time to heal," said Sandy.

"Very funny," Iggi grumbled. "Now, if you'll just stop laughing for a moment and stand me up, so I can pick up the nearest rock and throw it at that horse's-rear..."

The young centaur replied "Go ahead and try, elf," and he aimed an arrow in Iggi's direction.

"For crying out loud, for the last time, I'm not an *elf*, I'm a *fairy*," he replied, stomping his feet in anger and causing his tiny wings to flap wildly.

"Wait!" Replied Hope, eyeing the point of the arrow. "We mean you no harm. We just want to know why you attacked us."

"Attacked you?" Asked the centaur-boy quizzically. "You attacked me."

"We did not, saddle-sore. If you hadn't noticed, I'm the one picking thorns out of my rear," said Iggi.

Sandy replied, "Maybe there has been a misunderstanding."

She explained quickly what had happened to them as they arrived on the island. Iggi laughed at the idea.

"What are you laughing at, elf? Maybe the pretty girl is correct. Maybe we do have a miscommunication."

Sandy blushed at the centaur-boy's comment, for no one had ever called her pretty.

"What do you mean?" Asked Iggi, as he continued to pick thorns from the seat of his pants.

"Let me explain," the centaur-boy said, and told them what had actually happened. "My name is Cal and, as you can tell, I am a centaur. My sire is Optimus and my dam is Calla. We live just beyond the forest glade. Recently, I was involved in a yearly competition where the centaurs show off their skills. As you may not know, centaurs are known for their high intelligence and fierce competitive spirit. Until recently, I have always done extremely well in competition. This time, however, when I shot my first arrow, I missed the target completely. I was given a second chance and missed the mark once again. The elder centaurs felt something was amiss, as I have never done so poorly before. They called my sire and dam to the conference and they were questioned about the day's event. Centaurs are extremely honest and it was discovered that I was unfit. I suffer from a human defect that we had thought was long bred out of our human traits; I was found to be near-sighted."

"I do not understand," said Hope quizzically. "How did you do so well before, never having failed a competition?"

"That was the sad part. My sire, Optimus, discovered that my dam, Calla, in her love for me, would leave the competition early and when it was time for me to shoot, would knock my arrow out of the air and hit the bulls-eye dead center. She did this whenever I was shooting, which is why my secret was not discovered till now."

Hope, Sandy and Iggi looked at each other, thinking silently how their own people did the same for them, shielding them from those who would not understand. The power of love was indeed strong, especially that of a mother.

"What does this have to do with us being attacked by an arrow?" Asked Iggi, pulling the last of the thorns from his rear.

"I think I know," said Hope. "You were embarrassed and wanted to be alone and were practicing your archery in hopes of improving your skills."

"Yes," Cal admitted sadly. "I knew the other centaurs were in the village doing their daily chores, farming, building and making weaponry, so I asked my sire and dam if I could be alone to practice. They understood and allowed me to gallop off to practice, even though I knew no amount of practice would help...and that was when I was attacked by the elf."

Iggi gave Cal a dirty look and Cal corrected himself. "Fairy, I mean. I never expected anyone was nearby or I would not have fired my arrow haphazardly."

"That does make sense," said Sandy.

"Being strangers to your island, we mistook your practice arrow as an attack," Hope added.

"My sire and dam would be furious if they knew. They are always warning me about the danger of a misfired arrow," Cal replied.

"We understand," said Sandy, "And all is forgiven." Hope nodded.

"Wait just a gosh-darn minute," said Iggi. "You two weren't the ones being bucked off by donkey-boy and thrown into a briar bush."

"Oh, that," said Cal. "I do apologize for that, but our horse counterpart does not like to be ridden unexpectedly. Only when we are prepared do we accept that."

Iggi was not so quick to forgive, but Sandy gave him a look and he relented.

Cal added, "As is our custom, I would like to make up for this unfortunate incident by inviting you to our village for food and rest, if you are all agreeable to that."

Hope and Sandy accepted his offer readily, but Iggi asked if they had to ride him to the village.

Cal chuckled, "Of course not. I am too young and not as strong as my sire to be able to carry all three of you. You will have to walk of your own accord but it is not far."

Sandy was disappointed by this fact, for she had hoped to ride the centaur-boy; she liked his red hair and admired his physique, but she remained silent about this fact.

"Geez," yelled Iggi, "I almost forgot about Tuff," and he went to the briar patch where his little friend lay and placed him in his knapsack.

"Cute doll," Said Cal. "My sister would love to play with him."

"I don't think so, mule-face." Iggi quickly secured his little friend so as not to lose him.

As the three followed Cal, who was galloping quickly, they proceeded deeper and deeper into the forest until they arrived at a village. As Cal had said, the centaur-folk were indeed busy in their endeavors, which even included the foals. At first the adults were too busy in their efforts, but the children first took notice of the strangers. As the herd finally saw them, it was a young centaur-girl with auburn hair who shrieked,

"Cal."

The young filly was approximately ten years old, but was very fit in all the right places. She was busy stacking hay when she noticed Cal and galloped as quickly as possible to where the strangers were standing.

"Sienna, how is my favorite sister?" Cal asked.

"I am your only sister," she replied, "And who are these strangers? Or have your manners diminished along with your eyesight?"

Ouch, thought Iggi, who kept his thoughts to himself.

"Sorry," Cal said quickly, "Allow me to introduce them. The young lady on the right is Hope, a muse who lacks a talent, the sunbaked blonde on the left is Sandy, a mer-girl who is afraid of water, and finally, the one in the middle who looks like an elf, but is actually a fairy, is Iggi."

Ouch, ouch and triple ouch, thought Iggi, as he noticed the girls squirming when their defects were explained. Iggi's wings started to flutter uncontrollably as Iggi himself, who could not keep quiet, let out an insult of his own.

"Now that you know who we are, who're you? Don't tell me you're actually related to this donkey's-rear?" Sienna smiled, for as was her right as Cal's sister, she also liked to call him names.

"Yes, it is true, but I have all the looks." Iggi found that he could not agree more.

Sienna also noticed Tuff and quickly picked up the little rag doll. "My, what a handsome doll you are," she cooed to him. Iggi was quite surprised at her swiftness and within the blink of an eye, she was hugging Tuff and squeezing him to her bosom.

"He is so cute! Can I keep him?"

"No you can't," Iggi said rather angrily, then regretted his sudden outburst. For no sooner was Tuff safely back in his hands, than Sienna seemed awfully sad. Iggi, who had hidden his feelings for so long, could not believe how bad he felt at his rudeness and apologized to the young filly.

"Alright," he said, "You can't keep him, but you can play with him if you promise to be careful."

Sienna's eyes lit up,

"You mean you will let me play with him? Thank you, thank you." She gave Iggi a big hug and Iggi blushed as the young centaur-girl released him.

Cal shouted as his sister galloped away,

"Remember, you have to give him back."

"I will," she said, "I promise, and by the way, dam and sire are looking for you."

Cal waved at his little sister as she took off and turned quickly to his new friends.

"My sire and dam would be most interested to meet you and learn about your people. In exchange, they will provide you with the best hospitality you will ever find."

"Does that include grub?" Asked Iggi, licking his chops.

"You are impossible," said the girls in unison and Cal assured him it did.

"Let us go," Cal said and off they went.

The three strangers halfway expected the house to resemble a barn more than what it did resemble. It was a beautiful home that consisted of a compound of mud and straw made into concrete blocks. It was cool enough during summer, Cal explained, and sturdy enough to withstand a harsh winter. The enormous size was necessary due to their equine parts.

"That makes sense." said Hope, "Your people are obviously skilled craftsmen."

This time it was Cal who blushed red as his hooves scratched at something unseen on the ground. Cal would have continued to blush were it not for the fact that his sire and dam were coming to greet them.

"Cal, honey, where have you been?" Asked his dam. "Your sire and I were worried about you after…oh, pardon me, I did not see that you brought guests."

Cal's dam was a beautiful, middle-aged woman who looked much younger than she was. She had an auburn mane, which concealed her well-defined torso as she spoke. Sandy commented that she reminded her of her own mother, for obvious reasons. Cal's sire was a well-built centaur-man whose years of hard labor made him very muscular.

"Sire, dam, may I present Hope, Sandy, and Iggi. I ran into them while target- practicing. These are my sire and dam, Optimus and Calla, everyone." The two centaurs bowed their heads in acknowledgement, as did their guests.

"Cal, we are aware of where you met your friends," Said Optimus, as we found your arrow by a strange boat."

"Dam," said Cal, "I mean…"

"We will discuss this later," said Calla. "First, we must see to the comforts of your friends."

"Where is Sienna?" Asked Cal.

Optimus told him,

"Your sister is playing in her stall, serving tea to her doll."

"What?" Asked Iggi. "Where's her stall?"

"Cal, would you please show Iggi where your sister's stall is while we see to their dinner?"

Hope and Sandy volunteered to help Calla, who graciously accepted and directed her mate to attend to the fire as the night would surely be cold. Cal and Iggi soon arrived at his sister's stall and peeked in. As Optimus had said, she was indeed having tea and Tuff was dressed in a little suit. Iggi went ballistic.

"What have you done?" He stammered. "Tuff is not some doll you can dress at your whim; he's a boy."

"I know he is a boy," said Sienna stamping her hooves. "That is why he is wearing a suit."

"I want him back," said Iggi.

"You can have him back when we are done with tea," she retorted.

"Look you," Iggi said, but Sienna was not going to back down. "Besides," she said, "He likes it."

Iggi looked at his friend, who seemed no worse for wear, mumbled "Girls," and left the stall.

Cal knew his sister was demanding, but he assured Iggi that Tuff would be alright and after dinner, he promised she would give him back.

"Fine," Iggi said. "I just don't want anyone calling him Fluffy."

Cal smiled at this and escorted his new friend back to the kitchen, where dinner was being prepared. Hope and Sandy noticed that Iggi was quiet and did not question why. During dinner Optimus and Calla were able to learn a great deal about their visitors and the dilemma each faced. Sienna sat silently through dinner with Tuff seated by her side, staring at Iggi. When no one was looking she stuck out her tongue at him, which shocked him. After dinner, they all sat by the roaring fire and discussed each of their situations and that of their centaur-colt. The visitors learned that the centaurs had once lived in peace and harmony with humans until they realized the prejudices of such a pact. The humans used the centaur-males to help build structures while the females harvested crops and dealt with education. Finally, there came a point where the centaurs felt enslaved by the humans' laziness and rebelled against their oppression.

Calla gave her mate a stern look to warn him to tread carefully with his words, but he assured his mate that, as their guests were obviously not human, they should not be offended by such honesty. Still, his mate insisted on compassion when dealing with such ugly behavior. Optimus continued to relay their history and explained that, after much secret discussion, the centaurs decided to depart from human society forever and create their own society in which they could live together peacefully. Cal was bored with another history lesson because, as a young centaur, they were required to learn all about history in order not to repeat mistakes of the past, or so he was told by the elders. Being quite sure his new friends were equally as bored, Cal was about to change the subject. However, when he looked at the others, they showed great interest in his sire's lesson, so Cal remained silent. Hope knew that the centaurs had left humanity long ago, but never knew why, only that they preferred being solitary as opposed to living among humans. Hope knew that Clio, the muse of history, would be fascinated by this detailed information. Hope opened up the tome and found that it was indeed recording all it had learned, and she closed it again.

"What my mate failed to mention," interrupted Calla, "Is the fact that, although we do not mingle with humans, we are not so naïve to believe that without them we would still exist. However, for all our superior strength and intelligence, there are those among us who are prejudicial to these views and the subject is best left alone by proper centaurs. Human frailties have occurred only too recently, and that is why we are about to ask you for a favor."

"A favor?" Asked Iggi suspiciously. "What kind of favor?"

Optimus and Calla looked at each other and then at their colt; even Sienna, who was still mad at Iggi, hugged the little doll man to her bosom but remained quiet.

"My mate and I," said Optimus, "Are aware of each of your dilemmas and, had it been in our power to do so, we would surely have offered assistance. I fear, though, that it is not. We know you are seeking an end to your problems and would be much appreciative if you would help Cal. As is our custom, we do not put a price on our hospitality that is a given and we do not ask strangers for help. That is our way. We both feel this disability of Cal's will hinder him greatly among the others, forever reminding them of their need for humanity and that this will fuel their prejudices. We do not ask this lightly and the decision is yours alone to make, but we would be forever in your debt."

Hope and Sandy digested their request and agreed readily, as the young centaur-boy was expecting their answer to be "No," but as his sire and dam explained, it would have to be a unanimous voice because it affected all of them.

That left Iggi, who was looking at them as if they were all expecting him to say "No," but he just replied, "Whatever," which made the young centaur-boy leap into the air. "Just don't expect me to pick up after you," he said, referring to Cal's equine parts.

"No need to worry about that, fairy-boy," Cal replied, "I would expect no less from you. Once again, the group decided to spend the night, as they found it much easier to travel by daylight."

Optimus had prepared a quiver of arrows for his myopic colt, as this was the traditional gift from sire to colt. Calla prepared a fine meal of fruits and vegetables for him to take on their journey and hugged him to her warm bosom. Sienna even seemed envious of her brother's journey as she waved good-bye to him.

"Remember, donkey-boy, if you get lost, sire and dam always have me," and she giggled.

Optimus, Calla and Sienna waved farewell to the four as they arrived at the boat ready to set sail. The girls were the first to board the boat and sat down, making sure they were comfortable, as Iggi prepared himself the same way. Like Iggi before him, it was Cal who was uncertain of the boat's sea-worthiness as he tried to get on it. The swan boat rocked unsteadily, as if preparing for the added weight, as Cal tried desperately to gain footing. In a moment, he lost his balance, which was enough to send his equine rear down on the unsuspecting fairy.

"Get off me, horse's-rear!" He yelled. "I can't breathe." Iggi struggled to push Cal off of him.

"Stop that," Cal replied. "You are rocking the boat."

Finally, after much pushing and shoving, the boat was able to adjust comfortably to the added weight; Cal could see his sister giggling on shore.

"I told you, brother, that you were gaining weight," she called.

Cal, embarrassed, just sat down, making sure not to rock the boat again.

Iggi grumbled,

"I knew you would be more trouble than you're worth," and peered away at the open sea.

Cal tried to make conversation with Iggi, who seemed less flattened than he had moments before, but Iggi did not respond to his friendly overtures. The girls told Cal to ignore Iggi's mood swings, saying that sooner or later he would find something else to complain about. Sandy and Hope were more interested in finding out about Cal's problem and asked him in greater detail about his situation. Cal was hesitant about disclosing such human frailties, but being a centaur, he was honor-bound to be honest. Cal knew he had a problem seeing things as clearly as the other centaurs, but had always blamed it on the sun's reflected light.

Cal remembered that, as a young foal, he was only able to hit the target at two hundred paces or so; only when he was in competition was he able to increase his distance. Cal always found it strange and relayed the episode when he shot an arrow aiming for one target and it ricocheted off and knocked an apple out of his tutor's hand.

"The elder centaur thought I was showing off my skill and told me it was better to save my marksmanship for the competition. I was uncertain what had happened but did not want to antagonize the elder centaur any more than I had and quickly apologized to him.

The elder just shook his head and replied,

'It was great to be young,' and smiled as he made his way back to the village compound."

Sandy and Hope asked if that was when he first suspected something was wrong, and Cal nodded before he continued.

"I remember that day at the competition and how excited I was at preparing for the games. I wanted to show off a practice shot for my sire, but my dam, sounding very stern, said it was best not to waste such a valuable weapon.

'But dam,' I protested. But my dam was not to be swayed, and I obeyed her. As we made our way to the grounds, Optimus hugged me as any proud sire would and said simply,

'You are my colt and I will always be proud of you.'

I was waiting in line patiently as each centaur took his turn, and I looked to see where my family were sitting. The brightness of the sun hindered my view, but I was able to make out their outlines and waved to them. As always, my sister was uninterested in the competition, for she felt this was the males' way of showing off for their future mates. I had no interest in this ritual other than as a competition; my sire had won the respect of the centaur herd for his amazing accuracy, and my dam always said that was what had attracted her to him. The moment came when my name was read by the elders, and all the contestants watched in anticipation as I prepared my bow. I looked to the stands again and could make out my sire and sister watching me, but where was my dam? The centaur elders lost patience with me, for they were equally as excited about my performance. But rules were rules, and even I could not stall any longer.

I learned later from my family that, apparently, sire, sensing my uneasiness at not seeing my dam, excused himself and went looking for her. He thought maybe she needed to excuse herself; he galloped in the direction he had last seen her. After a few moments he came upon a bush and there before him was my dam.

How strange, my sire thought. Surely she has done what she intended to do. Why was she just standing there with an arrow ready? The answer was revealed quickly, for as I was taking aim two hundred paces or so away, my sire saw, with his own eyes, my dam preparing to shoot in the direction of the competition. Startled by this sight, my sire revealed his presence and asked my dam what she was doing. Having been discovered, my dam simply lowered her bow for a moment and said that what she did was done to prove that a dam's love has no bounds. Then she raised her bow again.

'Have you lost your horse-sense, my faithful mate?' My sire asked her.

'I do what I do for the love of my family,' she replied. 'As you suspect, dear mate, no colt can live up to his sire's expectations when he suffers from a genetic defect. You deny that which must be obvious even to you, that our colt's eyesight is poor due to a human frailty that we had long thought was bred out of our human counterpart. Is it our colt's humiliation you seek or the isolation that comes with being an outcast?" Tears started streaming down her face.

My sire suspected that I lacked visual acuity, but thought it would pass. But, never in all their years together had he seen his mate shed such tears. My dam was correct. My sire had denied what was certainly obvious for so long. I, his colt, lacked the keen eyesight of our kind.

'Forgive me,' my dear', my sire told her, trotting closer to his love, "But if our colt is to fail, is it not better to do so in front of those who love him?"

My dam quickly sheathed her arrow in its quiver and, as they galloped silently to where they had been moments before, they arrived just in time to hear the fateful arrow whirring through the air; both sire and dam waited for the outcome.

Sienna cried out,

'He missed,' and became suddenly excited by this turn of events in a competition that normally bored her. My sire and dam too had seen what my sister was referring to. Meanwhile, I simply stood stock still in horror at my error. The other centaurs were also equally amazed and they huddled together to discuss this strange occurrence. My sire saw that the elder centaurs were making their way to where I was standing, so he and my dam quickly came to my defense. Sienna, seeing where they were heading, decided this was too good to miss and hurried to me as the approaching elders arrived.

'He missed,' Sienna said to her sire and dam, but my sire waved her to be silent, and she knew better than to cross him. My dam, sensing what was to come, hugged Sienna, unsure if it was for Sienna's comfort or hers.

'Optimus,' said the brawny centaur elder, Chism, 'As you can plainly see, your colt has missed the target. Surely you find this as strange as we do.'

My sire knew better than to disagree with an elder, for they are chosen for their strength of mind and skill. Optimus himself was considered to be next in line to join the elders, but it was widely known that he detested politics and chose a simpler way of life.

'For the colt of Optimus, whose sire is known for his great strength and accuracy with a bow, to miss a target at two hundred paces, leads us to agree that sabotage is involved.'

The herd was commenting on what Chism had said and murmurs of agreement could be heard.

'May we examine the arrows?' Asked Chism. The other elders were already reaching for the quiver.

'We have no reason not to let you do as you ask, but in return we ask that this be done in a less public place,' my sire asked them.

The elders agreed readily to such a reasonable request, and my family and I were led swiftly to the village council, where there was more than ample room to accommodate us. I was scared as the elders watched me, but my sire and dam reassured me that things would work out for the best. I handed the elders my bow and quiver of arrows to examine.

'Cal, as you are aware, we suspended the competition due to your performance or rather lack of it, and are as confused by this display as you must be. We have examined your quiver and found the arrows to be of excellent quality, as these are the same arrows used by your sire and his sire before him to win many competitions. Have you any explanation for your lack of skill today, when so many times before you had showed such promising talent?'

I was silent, for I could offer no explanation as to why I lacked skill in practice, while in competitions, I excelled.

'I do not know, sir,' I told him, ashamed. 'The sun seemed brighter than usual.'

Chism looked at me. Obviously I was struggling to explain my poor performance, and because no centaur lied, Chism took what I said as truth.

'Maybe then,' said Chism, 'We might ask the same question of your family. Have you two any explanation for this startling event?'

My sire and dam knew that they could not deny the truth, as centaurs were forbidden to lie. So, as I stood by helplessly, I heard for the first time what had happened that day and in previous competitions. As my sire and dam explained why I had failed, I stood in awe, never suspecting how my dam's love for me could be so strong as to risk her being ostracized by the herd. The elders suspected this to be true, for they had noticed that just before my turn at competitions, my dam had so often disappeared. Now I, as well as the others in attendance, had discovered that I suffered from poor visual acuity, which had been unheard of since the beginning of the great cross-breeding. I was determined to be unfit and suffering from myopia like that of their human counterparts suffered. Long thought to be eradicated by their breeding with others of their kind, here it had appeared suddenly in a family of strong standing. After what seemed like hours, but was actually minutes, the elders' private discussion came to an end and my family stood bravely awaiting their decision.

'Cal, it is with deep regret and compassion for your family that we the elders of the centaur herd have no choice but to declare you unfit. Your disability is through no fault of your own, but stems from our weaker part, that which will forever remind us of our past. If we allow you to stay, we run the risk of a genetic throw back and, when the time comes to choose a mate, the risk of future generations. We, the centaur elders as a whole, have decided that from this moment on you will no longer be considered part of the herd and must leave the village at once.'

My sire and dam were shocked by such an obvious display of prejudice.

'Is there anything you wish to say before we disband this meeting? It is your right,' said Chism.

I spoke not for myself but for my family and the elders sat silent, listening to what I said.

'I have never denied that which is a natural part of me, but did not understand why I was different. I have always been proud of my centaur heritage, as I still am today, and would never do anything purposely to harm the herd. My sire and dam, especially, did what they did out of love, as any family would, but I alone will cause neither them nor you further embarrassment and so I accept your decision. I only ask that they not suffer any prejudice due to my disability and for making what they thought was the right decision on my behalf.'

My family later told me they were impressed by my bravery and honesty, and my willingness to sacrifice my life and happiness for that of my family and herd; they said they were never more proud of me than they were at that moment. The elders knew that I spoke from my heart, rather than from logic, but under these trying circumstances it was ignored by all. My sire thought that, despite the centaurs' reputation for fairness, how abruptly things changed when forced to deal with those very subjects. Had they forgotten so soon that the humans once treated them as nothing more than cattle, to be poked and prodded to do their bidding? This decision seemed to be hypocrisy at its finest.

As if reading my sire's mind, my dam simply responded,

'I agree.'

"So," Cal finished, "That is my story."

"How sad, as well as tragic," Hope replied. Iggi agreed, and Sandy seemed surprised by his revelation of feelings. Iggi thought silently how small his problem seemed when he compared it to others' misfortunes and was surprised himself at his show of feelings for the little colt.

Abruptly Iggi shouted out loud,

"Horses'-rears, all of them. Don't worry, hee-haw-boy. If you like abuse I'll always be here for you," and he laughed.

This seemed to cheer up Cal. For once since leaving his island, he actually felt like he truly belonged; day and night passed quickly as the four friends, strangers no longer, swapped stories about their lives. Hope was correct when she suggested they do that to let the young centaur-boy see that he was not alone, though they had all felt like they were at one time. Cal was fascinated by Iggi's story most of all and would stare at the fairy boy's wings whenever he was not looking.

"Stop that," Iggi said angrily if he caught Cal.

The girls thought he was arguing with his wings again but then realized he was looking at Cal.

"By the way, has anyone wondered why it's taking so long to get where we're going? If we don't stop soon, I'm going to have an accident," Iggi grumbled.

Cal asked Iggi why he did not just do it over the side. Iggi replied,

"Civilized people don't do that."

"Centaurs do," replied Cal. "Bodily functions are completely normal and we have no shame in that."

"That's why I said 'Civilized people,' not horses'-rears."

Sandy was about to step in to referee when Hope shouted,

"Look, an island."

The boys quickly forgot their argument and looked where the girls were pointing. The island was enormous by their standards, for as far as they could see, mountainous ledges loomed high and the terrain looked uninhabitable. As the others gaped at the immensity of the island,

Cal could only hope that for whatever reason the swan boat brought them here, they could find it soon and leave as quickly. As the boat swiftly prepared to dock, Cal could not help wonder what could live in such a hostile environment. As he turned his attention to the others, unbeknownst to him, his question was soon to be answered.

Chapter 9:

A HUGHE OF COLOR

The golden swan boat continued hurriedly to the massive island and as they gained speed toward their destination, Sandy could almost make out a shadow of huge proportions overhead.

"What is wrong?" Asked Hope.

"Nothing, I hope," replied Sandy. "For a moment I thought I saw something big land in the bushes, but I am probably just exhausted."

"Great!" Iggi said as he jumped off the boat, with the others following directly behind. "Not only do we have a mer-girl who's afraid of water, now we have one seeing things that aren't there. I'll prove to you we aren't going to find anything on this rock of an island except maybe boredom." Iggi grabbed a nearby tree branch and walked in the direction where Sandy thought she had seen something.

"Was it here," he said, shaking the stick angrily in the bushes.

"No," replied Sandy, "Not there."

"Was it here?" And once again he shook the bushes with the branch he held in his hand.

"No," she said, "It was right where you are standing."

"Be careful," cried Hope.

"I'm okay," he said. "I just want to prove that her nerves are shot from the long ride."

As Iggi once again shook the bushes, Cal shouted,

"Look out!" And Iggi was surprised to find the biggest, ugliest lizard staring him in the face.

"Oh my," Cal cried out, "A dragon!"

Obviously, the others were startled by this sudden sight; no human creature could exist in such rugged terrain. Only something that was much tougher could ever hope to live in such a barren land.

"What can we do?" Sandy cried in panic.

"Help," Iggi said as he ran into the clearing.

The dragon looked at the others for a split second, as if deciding which the best choice was and finally concluding that it was easier to tackle one than three, pursued the fairy swiftly.

"We have to do something," they said, while Iggi could be heard screaming as he disappeared from sight.

"You are a centaur," Sandy said. "Shoot it."

"In case you have not been listening," he said, "I do not see as well as normal centaurs."

"That is no excuse," she lashed out. "You are the only one carrying a bow and a quiver of arrows and so you are Iggi's only chance."

Cal knew that the mer-girl was correct, but he was sworn never to harm an innocent creature. Worse, he contemplated what would happen if he accidentally harmed Iggi with his bad marksmanship. Hope pleaded with the young centaur-boy to do something, anything was better than to have Iggi chomped to bits. Cal knew the muse was correct and with much trepidation, he armed his bow and galloped to where he could hear the fairy screaming. As Cal grew closer, he heard a terrible crashing sound as the bushes ahead were flattened mercilessly. The centaur came upon a clearing and spied the dragon, who had Iggi cornered beneath a ledge. Iggi looked petrified as he saw the centaur-boy standing at attention with bow in hand.

"Don't just stare, long-ears. Shoot already!"

As the dragon took a step closer to the fairy, Cal closed his eyes and fired directly at it. The arrow flew to its intended target and, half expecting it to pierce the dragon, Cal opened his eyes and saw the arrow bounce off the dragon's scales, hit the top of the ledge and by some minor miracle, cause the rocks above to crash down on the unsuspecting dragon. Realizing suddenly what was about to happen, the dragon scrambled for cover, but too late, as boulders bounced all around him and a huge one landed squarely on his tail. The dragon let out a cry of pain as the boulder pinned his tail to the ground. Hope and Sandy arrived just in time to see the dust bowl surrounding the three and blocking them from their sight.

"Is everyone alright?" Asked Hope nervously. "Where is Iggi?"

As the dust finally settled, Iggi could be seen crouching beneath the ledge, cowering with his hands over his face. Cal was shaken, for if Iggi had not been saved by this small miracle, he surely would have been chomped to bits or crushed by the fallen rocks.

"I am okay," said Cal as Sandy went to offer him assistance, "But Iggi may not be. Go see how he is doing."

Hope went to offer the fairy a hand, but Iggi was mumbling to himself if he was dead.

"No," said Hope with a smile, brushing the dust off him, "You are not dead, but you may well wish you were."

Iggi, confused by the event and still disoriented, finally realized what had just happened, regained his full faculties and started shouting,

"You idiot!" He yelled at Cal. "You could have killed me! Where are your brains, in your rear? Do you know how long it's going to take me to dust myself off?" As he said that, his wings started to flutter, trying to speed up the cleaning.

Sandy replied, laughing, "Things are back to normal. Too bad."

Cal was still shaken and apologized to Iggi as he and Iggi's wings brushed off the remaining dust.

"Here," said Cal and handed Tuff to the fairy, hoping this would make things right. "I am sorry," he said, "But you were in danger." We agreed that I had to do something."

Iggi shook his head, getting the rest of the rocks and dust out of his ears.

"Next time I need help, don't," he grumbled.

"What're we going to do with *him*?" Iggi asked.

The others looked at the dragon, who still remained pinned to the ground and they all noticed his most unusual color. Hope knew that dragons were enormous from what the other muses had said, but she understood that they were all one color. This dragon, which no longer seemed to be Iggi's attacker, but rather an innocent victim, looked like the spectrum of light. From the tip of his nose to the end of his tail he was a living rainbow. He was not as big as they had first thought, but his wings were of normal size. He seemed to be about twenty feet in length, rather small by comparison to the claims about dragons that she had read. Dragons were known for their ferocity, but these might just be rumors, although those who had encountered them were rarely seen again. According to legend, dragons were gifted with certain skills: fire-breathing and smoking, as well as telepathy. This creature might be able to tell them something of great importance; he seemed harmless enough as he sat there and whimpered helplessly.

Hope inquired from the others if they should try to communicate with him but was met with great resistance. Sandy was the first to speak.

"Hope, as much as I respect your beliefs, I cannot comfortably agree with this choice. He is a dangerous creature and it might be best to leave as soon as we are able."

"Cal, do you also feel this strongly?" Hope asked longingly. She did not even look at Iggi; she did not need to ask his opinion.

"I do," he said, obviously still shaken from the event. "I may not be as lucky as I was a few moments ago. It would be wise not to press our luck."

"But he seems all right," said Hope, risking an argument. "In fact, he seems rather tame and helpless."

"Tame?" Asked Iggi. "Helpless? Are you crazy? Was he tame when he attacked me and tried to chomp me to bits?" Iggi stormed closer to where the dragon sat helpless and told Hope he was not going to sit around while she tried to make this dangerous creature a pet. "The nerve," he said, and before Iggi was able to complete his last sentence, the rainbow-colored dragon swung his tail gently in Iggi's direction, barely touching him, which was enough. The next moment all Iggi could remember was a whirlpool of thoughts flooding his mind and the dragon seemed to speak.

Fairy, he said in a gentle voice, *do not be surprised by my knowledge of who and what you are, for I am not so great an adversary, as you are sadly mistaken.* Iggi sat helplessly as the violent whirlpool of thoughts became surprisingly calm. *My name is Hughe and I am indeed part of the dragon kingdom. Known for our great hunting skills as well as our longevity, we have been around long before humankind and most likely we will surpass them in the future.*

"Why are you telling me this, rainbow-snout? What does this have to do with me?" Asked Iggi. "Besides, you tried to eat me and don't think I've forgotten that," he said grumpily.

I will explain as best as I am able to in the short time I have and you will see exactly what this has to do with you as well as the others. As I have already stated, my name is Hughe, and I am of the dragon kingdom.

"Yes I know that, and quit breathing on me, what've you been eating, a horse?" Iggi eyed him suspiciously. "Say, what did you do with horse's-rear, did you eat him?"

Hughe chuckled, which only Iggi could hear, as they were connected telepathically.

No, I assure you I did no such thing, but mind you, I am quite hungry. Though to others of my kind there would be no question about eating habits, I am not like my brethren and am quite unique. I am a vegetarian.

Iggi was surprised by this fact but still eyed the dragon suspiciously. Hughe continued,

I was born fifty years ago and, although I am old by human standards, by dragon standards I am a mere hatchling. When I first hatched my parentals noticed the unique coloring of my scales when they reflected the sun and as I grew older they became even more apparent. Being born to the two oldest dragons in the kingdom gave me protection due to respect for my parentals, despite the fact that I had such a unique coloration. Most human-folk are aware of our reputation as fierce fighters, but few are aware that this is something that happens among us as well. There are those among us who look for the slightest reason to battle with others in order to gain hierarchy in the ranks. That is the challenge I face for myself and for those I love.

"What do you mean?" Asked Iggi. "What problem could you have that could be used against you?"

If you have not noticed, fairy, I am of unusual coloration and it is those who seek higher rank that are using my uniqueness against my parentals. Dragons are normally solid colors, such as red, green, blue, and orange, but it is my disgrace to be multi-colored and that isolates me from the rest. My parentals never questioned my uniqueness, and although even my siblings made discouraging comments, they were forced to accept it. Gap, the third-oldest dragon, felt that my coloring was a hindrance to the dragon kingdom and he sought out others for support in removing my parentals from the hierarchy. In front of the others, he challenged my poor skills at hunting and fire-breathing, as well as rampaging and telepathy. The others supported Gap out of fear of him, but silently remained loyal to my parentals.

'Prove to us he is worthy of the dragon name,' Gap told my parentals viciously. 'How can we expect leadership from those who would hatch such an offspring from obviously low-grade stock. It is obvious to those around him; he is a freak among his own kind.'

The dragons grumbled incoherently as Gap stood, proudly certain he had made his point. My paternal's eyes closed tightly as his anger swelled, just as my maternal showed equal ferocity towards Gap.

'Is it any better to be led by someone who lacks compassion for those of his own kind?' My paternal said baring his sharp teeth. 'Who among us has not realized for a moment how unique the dragon kingdom is compared to humankind? Uniqueness is a gift we are blessed with from the moment of our hatching and it is widely known, even among outsiders, that it is those differences that add to, not subtract from our strength. Mind you, Gap, you speak of low-level talents not being worthy of the name of the dragon, forgetting that you stand alone in third place while Hughes maternal and I stand proudly united before you as leaders in our community. We do this not out of desire as much as respect for those we proudly call brothers and sisters. Gap, even you must realize that to attack a hatchling who you claim is an aberration, leaves you in the position of last place, not third, as your title suggests.'

My maternal sat proudly in agreement with her mate's words for his hatchling as she continued to glare at Gap as only a maternal can.

'Whoever among you disagrees, speak now,' he finished. The dragons could be heard telepathically striving among themselves for answers.

'Gap is correct,' said one, while another said, *'But Hughe is unique,'* and a third said, *'And his talents are not up to par.'* Nevertheless, a vote was held and it was decided that, although my talents were weak, I deserved the chance to improve them and practice was surely what I needed. Gap was furious, for he had lost support. He slinked away before the meeting adjourned.

'I am sorry,' I said to my maternal, *'For the embarrassment I have caused our family.'*

'Do not fear,' said my maternal as she wrapped her wings around me. *'No hatchling of ours will ever be made to feel as if he does not belong, but the others are correct, great practice is needed.'*

So my paternal taught me how to fly at low-levels and hover above ground, my maternal taught me her technique of smoking so as not to be seen by prey or foe, and my siblings' shared their talents of rampaging, fire-breathing, and long-range telepathy. The latter, my parentals stressed, was *the most important so as to be able to avoid an unnecessary ambush. My talents did improve as my coloring became more apparent, but I was still considered a low-level practitioner. I was working on stalking telepathically, when my mind's eye caught wind of you and your companions. My ability is uncertain and so I came closer to you to find out more. That is when I saw the centaur with a quiver of arrows and thought we were being hunted. I can only use one talent at a time and had I continued to use my telepathy, would have known you meant no harm to me or the others. I had to make a quick decision as to what to do use my telepathy to probe the others or go after you, you were the safest choice, so I made my decision,* and Hughe concluded his long story.

"And you think scaring me out of my skin was the right decision, snoot-face?" Iggi shook his head. "Why didn't you just use your talent to read my mind then, instead of making me go through all of this?"

My talent does not work like that, I thought I said that. I have to be in close proximity and be able to touch you in order for it to work.

"Strange," Iggi said. "So what do you want from us, if you're not going to eat us?"

I was hoping you could help me find out about my uniqueness and perhaps help me find a place among my own kind, Hughe said pleadingly.

"Well," Iggi said, still not trusting the dragon. "I'd have to ask the others, but I can't do that unless you let me talk to them."

Of course, said Hughe, with a glimmer of hope in his eyes and in the next moment Iggi was once again himself.

Cal was preparing another arrow, while the girls looked in confusion at Iggi, who was recovering from his daze.

"Are you alright?" Asked Hope nervously.

"What do you mean?" Iggi asked.

"Sandy said one moment you were being chased by the dragon and the next moment you were staring into thin air. We should leave at once before he recovers," she added.

"I'm okay," he said, still shaking the confusion from his head, "But I don't think the salamander is dangerous. He wants our help."

"Help?" Cal said. "After he tried to eat you?"

Iggi understood his apprehension, but quickly explained what the dragon had told him, saying that in his trance-like state, the dragon, Hughe, was communicating with him and his actions were misunderstood "Kind of like we misunderstood you, Cal. Among his kind he is quite unique, not only in color but for his underdeveloped talents. He is desperate for help."

"Oh, poor thing," said Hope. "Of course we will help him, but first we have to get that rock off his tail."

The dragon understood their words and knew by their actions that they would not harm him, so he sat still as the three tried to free him.

"This isn't working," said Iggi. "He's too heavy."

"Maybe," said Cal, "We could hoist it off of him with some rope."

"Good thinking, nag-boy," said Iggi," But where would we find rope big enough?"

The others looked around and then glanced surreptitiously at Tuff.

"Forget it," Iggi said, noticing what they were looking at. "No way am I gonna risk Tuff."

Sandy replied quickly,

"It would not work anyway. Tuff's string is too small." Iggi smiled, as he was glad to hear it; then he came up with a better solution.

"Maybe we could use my-pretty-pony's quiver strap and have him pull while we push."

This time it was Cal who teased the fairy and said,

"Not a bad idea for a demented elf."

"I'm not an *elf*," said Iggi then realized he was being teased and finished,

"Whatever, let's just do it."

Cal took the strap off his quiver as the girls looped it quickly around the rock. As Cal pulled with all his equine strength, the others pushed as hard as they could. The rock started to sway but still was not moving, so Cal yelled for everybody to push harder…"And that includes you, dragon."

As the four pulled and pushed, the rock seemed to give way. Hughe thrust his tail upwards and the rock flew straight up. Iggi yelled and in a moment the dragon was free.

"Whew," the others said in unison, grateful that it was over. So was the dragon, who sat licking his wound. He was so happy he walked over and licked Iggi to say thanks.

"Stop that," Iggi said, "Or I'll push the rock back on you myself!" The dragon named Hughe just winked at him. Now that the others knew they were in no danger of being eaten, the girls went to Hughe and rubbed his snout, which seemed to cause him to purr.

"He is so cute," said Hope.

"Can he do tricks?" Asked Sandy.

"He's not a pet," Iggi said angrily.

"I think they know that," Cal said, "But girls are girls."

Hope and Sandy giggled as the dragon seemed to blush in all colors.

"What do we do with him now?" Asked Cal.

Hughe touched the fairy gently once again and Iggi heard him reply instantly that they should rest before resuming their journey. He knew where there were some wild berries and while they ate, he could ignite a fire to keep them warm.

The girls set up camp as Cal gathered sticks with which to start a fire. Hughe, although young, was able to set the bundle ablaze. He told Iggi he would fetch some berries that they could eat as they rested comfortably and off he went in search of food. As the others rested, falling asleep momentarily, they were awoken by a sudden rustling in the bushes.

"What was that?" Cal asked sleepily? Iggi was rubbing his eyes and raised his head a moment and said it was nothing, probably Hughe.

The sound became louder as the girls looked at where they had heard the noise first, but now it seemed closer. Sandy was startled by violent crashing through the brush and told the others it seemed to surround them.

"How can that be?" Asked Sandy, puzzled by the noise.

One moment it was in front of them and the next moment it echoed all around them as bush after bush was trampled before them, coming closer to where they were.

"Is that you, snoot-face?" Asked Iggi. "Still trying to be tough, are you? I'll show you," he said, while the others cautioned him to be careful. "I told you," he said rather bravely, "Hughe is a vegetablearian. He doesn't eat people." As Iggi went to where the loudest noise came from, the others quickly gathered together in a huddle. "Hey, you big iguana," Iggi yelled, "Show yourself. We know it's you. I can see your bloodshot eyes in the bushes."

Sandy said,

"But that is impossible. He is over there," and she pointed to the bush in front of her. As the others looked they too noticed big eyes watching them.

"That is impossible," Cal echoed. "I can see his tail poking out of the bush over there." As the others looked, they too noticed a tail protruding from the bushes.

"Wait a minute." Said Iggi. "If his tail is where Cal is and a pair of eyes is where I am and Sandy says she sees a pair of eyes in front of her, then that could only mean...Run!" He screamed.

The four tried to run, but it was too late, as three dragons pounced in front of them, blocking their escape. As the four stood horrified by what they saw, the dragons let out a roar of triumph at their discovery. The biggest of the dragons seemed to be the leader; he was at least fifty feet in length, green in color and flashing the biggest teeth. The others were smaller in size. One was about forty-five feet and red, while the other was silver; they were all licking their chops and drooling hungrily.

"Uh," said Hope, "We mean you no harm. We thought you were a friend of ours and we can see we were mistaken, so we will just leave." The green dragon looked at the others, which seemed to signal a command and the other two raised their wings to block any chance of the foursome's escape.

Leaving so soon? Said the leader of the dragons telepathically. *We would not dream of it. We were just going to have dinner. We rarely have guests for dinner,* he said, snarling as the others continued to lick their chops.

"Thanks, but we don't find the main course to our liking," Iggi said, "And besides, we're waiting for Hughe."

The dragons looked at each other and then at the strangers as the green dragon spoke. *How do you know Hughe?* He asked suspiciously.

"Go ahead, Iggi," Cal said as he pushed him forward, "Tell him and quickly."

Then Cal retreated to where Hope and Sandy were standing. Quickly, Iggi related the story of a few moments ago and the green dragon listened.

So you have agreed to help our little brother in his hour of need? But what makes you think you can help him, when you admittedly cannot even help yourself? The green dragon concluded.

Iggi's wings started to flutter uncontrollably, showing obviously that he was offended by the green dragon's words. Iggi's temper once again got the best of him.

"Listen here, you oversized newt, nobody with breath like yours and tail-rot is going to tell me what to do. You dragons consider yourselves all high and mighty, but when it comes down to it you're no better than anyone else. We're trying to help your brother and all you can think about is eating us. Tell me, did you actually fly in here or did you just roll on by and happen to find us sitting here?"

Iggi was tired and cranky and not even a dragon's threat was going to stop him. Cal, Sandy and Hope sat there, certain they were going to come to dinner as the main course whether they wanted to or not. Iggi just sat there with his arms folded, grumbling to himself about the green dragon.

The green dragon surprised the foursome by laughing out loud, or what they perceived as a laugh; it was really more like a snort.

Well said, fairy-boy, trying to get a rise out of Iggi, who strangely let it pass, *and bravely spoken. Rarely does any species take on a dragon, let alone three of the strongest, but occasionally we do get a human adventurer willing to risk his life to impress some lonely princess and live happily ever after. Mind you, bravery breeds stupidity. We only attack when necessary to protect ourselves, but occasionally we do get bored and play the fearsome creature for dramatic purposes. In the end, everyone is happy, although occasionally there are accidents.*

Hope, feeling more confident that this dragon's words were sincere, asked, "Do you really eat people?"

Hmm, once again our reputation precedes us, he laughed and replied, *no. Human species do not agree with our constitution. Besides, it is much harder to eat something that talks back.*

Sandy spoke up, having been silent throughout the conversation. "But you said accidents occasionally happen."

Words are often misunderstood. I was referring to the clumsy knight dressed in full armor trying to balance a huge sword. It is amazing we can even stop ourselves from laughing, as he bravely declares his love for the kingdom and swings clumsily. Or the adventurer whose ego gets a little too much bruising and, rather than face embarrassment before his people, chooses to reside forever in the next village.

"So his people think he died bravely and his reputation remains intact," said Cal.

Yes, quite astute, centaur. I have met many of your kind and have always respected their intelligence.

Cal's chest swelled with pride at hearing the dragon's comment and for once in his life he never felt more proud of his heritage. The two dragons raised their snouts in the air and telepathically told the green dragon that Hughe was approaching. As Hughe made his appearance, he failed to notice the other dragons as his mouth was filled with branches bearing fruit, but as he came closer their scent was unmistakable. He released the fruit-bearing branches and immediately put himself between his new friends and his siblings and faced them down. Smoke rose from his nostrils as his eyes narrowed, waiting for a fight that never came.

Hello little brother, the green dragon said as the other two snorted their hellos. No need to fear, little brother. We have no desire to harm your playmates.

Hughe looked at the foursome, who did not seem worried and he ceased his aggressive posturing. The oldest of the dragons was the first to rub his wings gently around his sibling as the others joined in. Hope, Sandy and Cal sat, enviously remembering their own families and how much they missed them. The green dragon opened the lines of communication between all of them by telepathically linking them together. Hughe, being young, was only able to do this with one at a time and only when he touched someone, so the green dragon made the process much easier.

Hughe asked eagerly about his parentals and what was happening at the council and his brothers relayed the events. Gap was becoming ever more burdensome, as was his readiness to speak his mind. Their parentals still had support, but even the most loyal were beginning to have doubts. His brothers were actually sent to find Hughe and bring him home, but Hughe resisted this idea. He felt he had to prove his right to exist as himself and told his brothers of his adventure. The green dragon huffed and puffed but Hughe was more certain this would be best for all and would give his parents a chance to take care of Gap without any distraction. The other siblings agreed finally and it was decided that Hughe would be given the chance to find his place in life.

"See you later, claw-toe, and don't forget to gargle," said Iggi in parting.

The green dragon replied as they were rampaging back through the forest, *I may see you for dinner after all.* He laughed once more and was gone.

"Whew," said Cal, "That was close!"

"For once I agree with you, bit-boy," said Iggi, as did the girls from the look on their faces.

"But what are we to do now? Iggi asked.

Sandy was the first to speak after their encounter.

"Maybe we should do just what we are doing already and that is to continue."

"Continue with what, fish-tail? We don't even know what we're supposed to do," Iggi said irritably.

Hope agreed, and reminded them that whatever they were supposed to do, at least it brought the five of them together and it was better than what they could do alone.

"You know, for a talentless muse you're pretty smart," Iggi said, and his wings concurred by way of fluttering.

"What is it Hughe?" Asked Hope and touched the dragon gently so they could communicate.

What if our chance meeting was not quite by accident? I feel like we are being herded into something that will challenge us all and without each other's talents we will certainly fail.

When Hope told the rest what Hughe had said, the group looked at each other and then at the little dragon. All were at a loss for words.

Dawn once again came swiftly as the others prepared to board the boat; Hughe himself was amazed at the beautiful swan boat, for he had never seen anything quite like it.

Is this magic? Hughe asked, and being in close proximity to the others, he was able to communicate his words to all of them.

"Yes, of a type," Hope said, and explained about the boat's immediate magic and the illusion of animation and for what purpose.

Truly amazing, he smiled with toothy admiration and the boat, sensing his thoughts, blushed a deep red.

Although the others were seated quite comfortably by the boat's ability to adjust to the extra weight and size of its passengers, nevertheless Iggi had complained about Hughe's breath and Cal's tail-swishing in his face, but in not such kind words, while the girls amused themselves at seeing his predicament.

"Get your big rear off me," Iggi said to Cal.

"I am trying. Quit pushing me," Cal replied. We should have let the dragons eat you, either before or after they shriveled your wings to nubs, fly-boy and used Tuff to floss their teeth.

Hughe smiled as best he could for a dragon but his thoughts were occupied with adjusting himself in the boat, where his tail was curled into a ball. Hope and Sandy both reassured Hughe that this was normal for the boys and after a while you just learned to ignore them.

As Sandy kept watch, uncertain of where they were now headed and wondering if the boat could accommodate any more passengers, Hope opened up the tome her sister Clio had given her and saw that everything that had transpired was being recorded exactly. She closed her eyes and wondered what might happen next. The boat sailed continuously as it had done so many times before; night turned to day and back into night again and still the boat continued on. Hope had loved the boat from day one when she first caught sight of it and was quite used to it by now. However, the others were starting to show signs of sea-sickness when the sea became rough and wave after wave crashed all around them. Sandy had an especially hard time. As brave as she tried to be, she could not help feeling fearful of the water from which she was born. Hope had almost forgotten about her problem because, of all of them, hers was the least noticeable until they were, as Hope felt, safely on the boat. Waves crashed endlessly around them as Sandy bravely faced her fears that they might drown.

As the boys were distracted by what they were seeing around them,

Hope thought that maybe if Sandy had something to hold on to, it might make the trip that much easier. Hope looked inside her bag, rummaging through it to see if there was indeed something that could give Sandy courage; she found the compass, star map, telescope, some herbs, a book on plants and a lyre. The latter was always calming to those who heard it, but she did not think that it would work in this case. She looked at the others and tried hard to remember what each of them had brought on the journey. Cal had a quiver of arrows that might come in handy later but for now was useless. Sandy herself brought some shells, but Hope thought those would just remind her more of what she feared. Hughe, small by dragon standards, but large when compared to the others, had only recently brought branches carrying fruit and Iggi... hmm, she thought, Iggi had brought the one item he valued the most, something that was made by him out of love and provided him courage and comfort. That was his little friend, Tuff. Hope looked at where Iggi had fallen asleep and was amazed how anyone could do that so easily in weather such as this. Nevertheless, it surely was because his little friend helped him cope in all situations.

"Iggi," Hope whispered so as not to disturb the others, but Iggi did not wake up; he simply turned on his side. No use, she said as she looked at Sandy, who was holding her stomach as she looked over the side of the boat. Hope was taught from an early age that it was wrong to take anything that did not belong to you without the person's permission, but this was an emergency, she told herself and slid over to where the rag doll was peeking out of his confinement, his eyes meeting hers, or what looked like eyes, but were actually tiny beans sewn on his face. No matter how one moved in any direction, the eyes seemed to follow them precisely. Hope opened the bag and retrieved the little man gently. She told him of her actions and hoped he would understand. Hope was surprised for the second time when, for an instant, she could have sworn she saw a glint of understanding in the black eyes, but again she shrugged this off as a trick of the light. Iggi was still fast asleep as Hope raised Tuff in her hands and climbed over to where her friend Sandy was sitting.

"What are you doing?" Asked Sandy quizzically. "Iggi will get really upset."

"That is probably true," said Hope, "But it is important to help you feel better and I thought Tuff might take your mind off this boat ride. Anyway," Hope said as she giggled, "Iggi always ends up forgetting why he was mad in the first place," and then it was Sandy's turn to giggle. "As long as you are careful with him, I am sure he would not mind."

But the girls knew better. Sandy promised she would indeed be careful with him and she held the little rag doll close to her, admiring his unique detail, the way his arms and legs moved by joints much like a real person. As she hugged him to her bosom, she felt the warmth of his tiny little body and she finally understood why Iggi liked him so much, as her feelings of fear simply vanished.

"You are so cute," she told Tuff. "I would want someone just like you to talk to. You are so patient and understanding," she smiled. Hope was so preoccupied with the empathy that these two shared that she failed to hear the honk of warning from the boat until it was too late.

"What is wrong?" Hope asked the boat, but it just kept honking in quick short bursts and then Hope realized what it was trying to warn them about.

"Oh no!" Screamed Sandy. "There is a rogue wave and it is heading directly for us."

The swan boat paddled faster, trying to escape the inevitable. The others awoke to the chaos just in time to see the wave, which was as wide as it was high, come toward them like an unstoppable juggernaut. The others braced for impact as the wave came crashing down on them and capsized the swan boat, throwing all of them into the sea.

"Hang on!" Shouted Cal, as he grabbed desperately at the boat, using his muscles to pull himself up, while the others; Hope, Iggi and Hughe tried just as desperately to do the same. Hughe's body, although small, was the heaviest. Still, he was amazingly buoyant and was able to support the weight of Hope, Iggi and Cal when they grabbed his tail, holding on for dear life, until Cal, using all his equine strength, was able to hoist himself up into the boat, and then pull in the others, Hughe by his tail. Coughing and sputtering was heard all around the boat as they tried to clear their throats of the salt water.

"Is everyone alright?" Asked Hope, choking out the words and the salt taste from her mouth.

"I think so," said Cal and Hughe nodded agreement while blowing water out of his nostrils.

"What, no words from fish-tail? What's a matter, did you get water-logged?" Then Iggi noticed what the others did; Sandy was nowhere to be seen.

"Sandy, oh no," cried Hope, as salty tears streamed down her face. "Where is she?"

Iggi was as shocked as she was, for he remembered waking up and seeing that she was holding Tuff, and then the rogue wave hit and they all went everywhere. Iggi had seen his best friend floating away on the currents and heard briefly as Sandy screamed,

"I have to get him!" And then he was being dragged by Cal, who told him to grab his tail and he would try to swim to Hughe.

"Why, why, why?" Iggi asked over and over, as the others realized what had happened. But Iggi knew exactly why she had done it.

"After all," he said, "I'm the one who fussed and fretted about Tuff all the time. So she sacrificed herself for my best friend," he said, as the others sat shaken. "It's all my fault," he said and, for once, salty tears were streaming down his face.

"No," said Hope. "It was my fault; I am the one who gave her Tuff because she was so afraid, and now I have lost both of them."

"No," replied Cal. "Had it not been for the fact that I am near-sighted, I would have seen she was in trouble."

Hughe touched him and he relayed his message. *If he had been a*

*more powerful dragon, he could have saved them all, but in the end we all
lost them.*

The boat sailed on while the foursome sat silent.

Days later, the mood was still somber. They sat silent still, in shock
from the past events. Cal had offered the others some fruits and nuts,
but they barely picked at the food he gave them. Cal could not blame
them for their lack of appetite as he himself was not hungry. Still, he
told them that if danger approached them, they would need their full
strength for the challenge. Hope nodded agreement, as did the rest;
although they ate barely enough to sustain them, it was a start. Iggi,
who was usually grumpy, paid no attention when his wings started to
flutter as if to distract him from his mood. Instead, he just ignored
them and they fell still. Hope had asked Hughe if it was possible to use
his telepathy to find Sandy and Tuff, but even though he knew it was
impossible, he tried his best to do as she asked. Hughe concentrated
as he had seen his parentals do and scanned wide for any sign of life
from Sandy and Tuff, but came back empty, depressed even more at
his underdeveloped talents. Cal had even suggested he could fly, as he
had more powerful wings than Iggi, but he simply shook his head, no.
He had thought of flying, but even the most powerful dragons needed
ground on which to gain speed. Truly, he felt useless.

"You did your best," said Hope as she rubbed the multi-colored
dragon's nose, which made him feel a little better but not much. They
just had to face it; they would never see their friends again.

"I'm tired of this," said Iggi, sounding like his old self again. "Yes, I
miss them. "We're all unhappy, but we have to go on. If we don't, their
sacrifice will be for nothing."

Hope, Cal and Hughe looked surprised at Iggi's sudden maturity; as
cold as it sounded, it was very true. It made perfect sense; Sandy would
want them to go on without her, as the others would expect her to go
on without them. Hope just did not know why it had to be this way.
Surely, Delphi should have seen this beforehand, should have warned

her at least. No, thought Hope sadly, what was it her sister Clio had said to her before she left, that she was responsible for her own destiny and must take responsibility. Had she known, would she have still chosen to take the risk?

Hughe sat silent, sending out his thoughts into the vast sea, for what purpose he did not know, but he felt he had to continue to try. He kept silent due to the concentration it took for him to exert such force, unsure if the effort was even worth it. He glanced in one direction and felt nothing and then he looked to the side from where they had come and felt nothing as well. Wait, he thought, what was that? It was a small tug in his mind, like that of direct contact, but surely it could not be, so far away from civilization. Hughe shrugged this off as simple fatigue and scanned in the direction the boat was now facing. Nothing, he thought as he slumped down into a ball.

Chapter 10:

THE BIGGER THEY ARE

As the swan boat prepared to dock, all eyes were on the new island. The lush vegetation, masked only by its size, was a virtual paradise. Its trees bore strange, colored fruit that remained unplucked, still ripening on the branches. They saw plants with vines as thick as tree trunks, growing steadily around them, with buds of strange and wondrous flowers that none of them had ever seen. Hope could not help but wonder at how such beauty could grow unattended in such a desolate location along the sandy shore. Hope thought how perfectly planned it all seemed, like someone's own personal garden, but even Hope knew that was absurd. What could have created this perfection, or the better question was who? Hope's next thought was interrupted by Iggi's overwhelming enthusiasm.

"You can all sit here gawking at each other, but as for me, I'm starving and I've been on this boat way too long. It's time to eat."

And off he marched toward the orchards they had seen.

Cal yelled "Wait," and tried to grab Iggi, but it was too late, for as soon as Iggi reached one of the trees, he began to throw rocks at the fruit, trying to knock one down. By the way he was standing with his arms folded, Hope could see that the centaur-boy seemed tense and asked him,

"Is something wrong?"

Cal replied, "It could be nothing, but would it not be more logical to learn where we are and determine if it is safe first before we foolishly end up on the wrong end of the stick…again?"

"What do you mean?" Asked Hope.

Cal explained, "We are strangers here and do not know the local botany. I feel the logical choice would be to scout the island first to see if it is inhabited and to test anything that looks edible to see if it is safe. I assure you I am as hungry as our friend, but my equine senses prohibit me from taking any action to alleviate it that might cause me to make an irrational decision."

Hughe, whose ears were perked up, was listening to what the centaur-boy was saying, and though he was unable to speak directly, he used his telepathy in order to be heard. After he made direct contact with Hope by touching her with his tail, he told her that he agreed with Cal.

"Then how are we to test the food that we find, unless one of us eats it?" Asked Hope.

Hughe sent his thoughts to her. *I believe that if I am able to get a sample, I am almost certain I would be able to sniff out whether it was edible.*

Hope was uncertain what to do. She also was very hungry, as they had lost most of the food when they capsized, and she remembered what her indecision had cost them: two best friends. Hope looked to where Iggi was standing and saw him desperately trying to retrieve a fruit from the tree. Try as he might he could not get it and he was equally irritated at his wings for their constant buzzing. She overheard him yelling at his wings to stop and complaining how little help they were to him, all the while throwing rocks at the fruit, trying to knock down at least one. No, she thought, if she was to be their leader she had to make a decision fast, hoping that in the process no one else would get hurt. How? She thought silently, forgetting the link she and Hughe shared.

If I may make a suggestion, Hughe told her silently, *maybe the centaur-boy could clip one with an arrow.*

That thought had crossed her mind, she told him, but what if he missed the apple and hurt one of them accidently?

Then we must take precautions to make sure that does not happen, he replied.

Hope immediately broke contact with Hughe and asked Cal if this was at all possible. Cal assured her that it was, provided he was close enough to his target. The three walked over to Iggi, who was still struggling and still having no luck. Iggi stared at them as they approached him.

"What?" He demanded.

"Move aside," Cal said. "I am going to try to shoot a fruit from the tree."

"Really?" Said Iggi. "Wouldn't it be easier if you just aimed for the tree?" He said with a grin.

Cal, not to be bested, replied, "I could just practice aiming at you. Anything that big even I could not miss."

"Uh, just shoot already," Iggi said, for he was not certain Cal was joking.

"Now that it is settled, would everyone mind moving behind me. A wild arrow can be just as dangerous," Cal said.

Hope and Iggi remembered when they had first met Cal and decided to hide behind Hughe for better protection. Hughe figured out what they were doing. Everyone knew dragon-hide was tough, even that of young dragons, but it was best not to press their luck. He arched his back to provide even more security. Cal saw everyone was amply protected; he squinted to center the target, drew his bow and fired. The arrow flew swiftly and struck the branch where the strange fruit was hanging; made a plink sound, and the arrow fell directly below the tree.

"You burro-breath," yelled Iggi, "You missed! Donkey-boy missed. Big surprise; you couldn't hit the side of a mountain," he raged. Iggi was not through with Cal. He marched to where the tree was and pointed, "tree, fruit, tree, fruit, what part of that didn't you understand?" Asked Iggi, shaking his head.

"But I could not miss. I was not aiming for the fruit," Cal replied.

"You did your best Cal, but that is all we could ask you to do. I was not hungry anyway," Hope said.

Cal said again, "I told you, I was not aiming for the fruit. I was aiming for…" and before Cal could finish his sentence, Iggi, who was standing beneath the tree, heard a snap and the fruit-laden branch landed on Iggi's head. Iggi fell to the ground with a thump, and then sat up, rubbing his head.

The others tried their best to refrain from laughing out loud, but were unsuccessful and Iggi just told them to be quiet. Cal offered Iggi his hand, but the fairy was fuming and simply grumbled as he got up.

"How come I'm always the one getting hit on the head?" He asked, still rubbing his head, where the others could see a bump was forming.

"Just unlucky, I guess," said Cal over his shoulder as he trotted away. Iggi grabbed the fruit and held it in front of Hughe's snout.

"Just don't get dragon slobber all over it," he said.

"He is not going to eat it," said Hope. "He only wants to sniff it to see if it is poisonous."

"Poison. On second thought, I'm not as hungry as I thought I was," said Iggi in disgust.

Hughe sniffed the strange fruit and sniffed it again just to be sure; it smelled like an orange but was crimson like an apple, only much bigger. Hope touched Hughe's snout and asked if it was okay to eat.

Hughe told her, *I believe the fruit is edible but I cannot be certain of the taste without first trying it. Would you like me to do that? I believe it will nourish us.*

"No, that will not be necessary. I trust your instincts," Hope said.

She told the others the fruit was safe to eat and asked Cal to knock down some more. Iggi, having heard this and not wanting to wait, devoured the fruit most appreciatively, as was evident by the fibrous strands on his face.

"Mmm, mmm," he said as juice spilled out of his mouth.

The others chose a more polite way of eating by using one of Cal's arrows to slice it into pieces. After they were full and felt completely rested, Cal suggested that maybe it might be best to scout the area for hidden danger, but from a bird's eye view, to be more precise. Cal asked Hughe if he was up to the challenge and the dragon readily agreed.

I am young, he said, *but I believe the nourishment has sustained me enough to attempt flight. And I must concur with Cal's logic. Even among dragons, the centaurs are known for their unquestionable skill of strategy and high-intelligence.*

This caused Cal to blush, for he was not used to such compliments and thanked the dragon. It was not meant as a compliment, but a fact and Hughe said,

You are welcome, and gave Cal a wink. *However, I do see a problem, though it is no fault of Cal's, but of my own. I am still a novice and have not had much practice in flight and therein lies the problem. If I am to succeed, I will need to concentrate on matters and will be unable to view the surroundings.*

"Do you have any suggestions?" Asked Hope.

It might be best if I took along a companion, one who could freely view the area so I will not be distracted from the task at hand, Hughe said.

"That is an excellent idea, but which one of us?" Asked Hope quizzically.

The smaller the person, the easier it would be to maintain flight. That way I would not have any distractions.

"You mean me?" Asked Hope. Hughe sensed the muse's fear and assured Hope that he did not mean her.

As much as I am certain you would enjoy the experience of being airborne, regrettably that cannot be for the simple fact that my hide is tough and might cause some discomfort to your, um...

Hughe was searching for a delicate word to describe what he meant, but Hope, seeing Hughe fumble for words, caught on to what he meant.

"You mean my posterior," said Hope, trying not to giggle.

Yes, he said, and blushed a deep red.

"Then which one of the boys?" Asked Hope.

Hughe replied, *I have thought long and hard about this and could only come up with one logical choice. Iggi would be the perfect companion. His people are already adapted to the wonders of flight but even though Iggi himself is grounded, he fits the required measurements. I think he is the perfect choice.*

Hope rubbed Hughe's snout. "What if he refuses?" She asked.

I am certain he will make a drama out of the whole thing, but that is a charade. Iggi will not turn down our request for help because even though he will be assisted, in his mind flying is flying and so he will go along with our request.

Chapter 11:

FLIGHT OF FANCY

H ope and Hughe returned just in time to hear Iggi and Cal yelling back and forth at each other.

"You did that on purpose," shouted Iggi, as his wings buzzed crazily.

"I did no such thing. Besides, you yelled "Giddy-up," Cal said, stomping his hooves on the ground. "Have you ever thought that the real reason you cannot fly is because you are too fat?" Cal asked.

"Turn around and say that, so I'm not speaking to the wrong end," Iggi yelled back. Then he said, "What's the use. I'd be mad too if my father was a gelding," he laughed.

"Oh yeah?" Cal said. "Come over here and say that, so I can squash you like the gnat you are," said Cal as he grabbed a branch with which to swat him.

"Here, I'll move closer so you can see me," Iggi snorted.

Hope could see Cal bucking like a wild bronco, as Iggi poked and prodded him with Cal's own arrow.

"Stop it at once!" Shouted Hope. "You are both acting like children."

This sudden outburst startled the two boys and they stood before her open-mouthed.

Iggi: "He started it. He hit me purposely on the head again with another fruit."

Cal: "I did not! You told me to "Giddy-up.""

Iggi: "Did not."

Cal: "Did too."

This was getting nowhere fast, thought Hope and finally she said,

"Enough is enough. One more outburst and Hughe and I will get back on the boat and leave you both here to sort out your differences." Hope was bluffing, but they were not certain what would happen if they challenged her. Hope's only advantage was the fact that her frustration sounded like anger, but would it be enough, she wondered. Iggi and Cal looked at each other than lowered their eyes; her bluff had worked.

"I am sorry," said Cal as he shuffled his hooves.

"Yeah, what he said," Iggi replied.

Hughe just chuckled to himself so as not to be heard by the boys.

"What's the plan?" Iggi asked as if nothing had transpired.

Hope explained that Hughe was going to scout the island from the air, but that he felt bringing along a companion might be best so he would not be distracted.

"That is why we need one of you to help," said Hope.

"Which one of us?" Asked Cal.

Hope, not wanting to hurt the others' feelings, explained in logical terms Hughe's reasons for choosing Iggi.

Upon hearing this, Iggi said, "Me?"

"Yes, you," said Hope, and explained why he was the most logical choice. Cal, who looked disappointed, analyzed the choice in his mind and could not find fault in Hughe's reasoning, so he said,

"I agree. Centaurs are well suited for the land, but in flight our body structure would obviously prove a hindrance and so your logic is perfect, Hughe." He nodded at the dragon.

Iggi could not hide his excitement and without thinking, hugged the centaur-boy.

"When do we leave, huh?" Asked Iggi, trying to regain his nonchalance.

Hughe, who was listening to what was being said, simply lowered his back and spread his wings.

"Now," said Hope.

Climbing a dragon isn't easy, thought Iggi, but with Cal's assistance, he was finally able to hang on to Hughe's neck. The sand proved too soft for Hughe to get a running start, as his weight, along with his passenger's, caused them to sink. Hughe suggested that maybe the ledge above them would provide him with more stability and enable him to get a running start. Folding his wings, Hughe and Iggi climbed high upon the rocky ledge as Cal and Hope waited down below. Shielding their eyes from the bright sun, they continued to watch as Hughe and Iggi climbed higher and finally rested on the ledge.

"Can you see them?" Asked Cal, who was trying to get a glimpse of them but at that distance could only see shadows. Cal squinted as he barely made out two looming shadows and what he perceived could only be Hughe and Iggi. The smaller of the shadows had to be the fairy-boy because he could see it waving its hands wildly, trying to get their attention; by process of elimination, the other had to be Hughe. As Cal tried to focus his eyes once again, the bigger shadow seemed to be blinking in and out of focus. One minute he was there and the next minute gone. Cal rubbed his eyes and could only compare what he was seeing to that of an ember about to be extinguished. At first, Cal thought it might be a trick of the light, but then his fears deepened as he attributed it to his defect. Saddened by this thought, Cal could only look to where Hope was pointing. There was no point in worrying her, he thought, as the shadow continued playing its game.

Hope had trouble at first seeing the pair due to their height as the dragon scaled the mountain skillfully with his enormous claws and Iggi clung on for dear life until they were finally resting on the ledge overhead. Hope shielded her eyes, as she barely made out the pair and realized they had reached the top. Hope also saw Iggi waving his hands wildly as he whooped and hollered in his eagerness to fly. It was only when she tried to make out Hughe, was she surprised at what she saw, and or rather did not see. She saw the duo as they made it to the ledge that stood high above them, where the smaller shadow continued to wave at them. But the moment Hughe's multi-colored scales came into direct contact with the sun, he seemed to fade, gradually at first as he became brighter and brighter and then, like a light suddenly going out, he was gone. To Hope it looked as if Iggi had mastered the art of flying, or hovering as it were, but she knew this was not just improbable, but impossible.

Hope shook her tiny head and told herself that she must truly be tired, surely that must be it. Still Hope wondered as she looked to the pair again and saw Hughe as clear as day. Best not to worry Cal, she thought, as she looked once again to where the dragon was preparing to take off. Hughe, with Iggi astride him, eyed the land beneath as if he was calculating the distance he needed to accomplish his flight.

"Are we just going to stand here all day taking in the sights?" Exclaimed Iggi. "Let's get on with it," he said excitedly.

Patience, said Hughe, *patience. I cannot simply leap from this distance without proper planning, for it could be disastrous*, he said.

"What're you going to do?" Asked Iggi nervously.

Hughe cocked his head toward Iggi and said,

Take a leap of faith, and chuckled.

"What? Are you crazy?" Asked Iggi. "We won't make it!"

Hughe shook his head and told him, *I believe we will indeed make it, provided we have a running start. The problem is that I cannot be certain of the distance that is required for such an action. I have only experienced flight a few times before, preferring safer ground.*

Iggi shook his head in disbelief.

"Yadda, yadda, yadda, blah, blah, blah, so what're you saying? We would have been better off if we just let your brothers eat us?" He asked.

Hughe usually ignored such prejudices but told the fairy,

If you do not be quiet so I can concentrate, you just may find out why fairies, as well as the human species, disagree with a dragon's constitution.

Iggi gulped at hearing this, said,

"Whatever," and then fell silent.

After a few minutes, Hughe asked Iggi if he was prepared.

"Prepared for what? To go splat?" He asked.

Hughe simply replied,

Maybe to just go bounce, and chuckled.

Iggi closed his eyes but made sure he was hanging on tight and in the next moment he felt a rush of air as the dragon ran with great speed and leapt off the mountain with wings spread. Hope and Cal looked on in horror as the two leapt off the cliff. Downward they fell like a rock.

Iggi could be heard screaming,

"Fly you big, dumb lizard, fly!" As they continued to plummet out of control toward the ground below.

"Oh no!" Shrieked Hope. "They are going to crash," and she covered her eyes, waiting for the inevitable.

Cal looked and as he saw the dragon struggling to gain control, he also felt certain that they were headed for doom. As Cal prepared to cover his own eyes, he was amazed to see Hughe miraculously spread his wings to the fullest and soar back into the sky when the two were only moments from certain disaster.

"Look, Hope!" Yelled Cal, struggling to pry Hope's hands away from her face. "Look!" He repeated.

Cal could not believe what he saw as he continued to struggle to get Hope to open her eyes. Hope finally gave in and compromised by opening just one eye. She fully expected to see something horrible and tried to steady herself. Hope was amazed and relieved to see that her fears were unfounded as she watched Hughe and Iggi soaring ever higher into the sky, gaining altitude while the fairy waved at them.

"Yee hah," whooped Iggi as he waved at them before the two disappeared from sight.

"They did it!" Yelled Cal, as he pranced from side to side.

"They sure did," said Hope and, in her excitement, gave the centaur-boy a hug. Cal hugged her back.

High above the clouds, Iggi could not hold back his excitement and, as his tiny wings buzzed happily in agreement, he yelled,

"You did it, rainbow-sprite, I knew you could," and he let out another holler.

Hughe, on the other hand, let out a sigh.

We did it, he said and, for the first time since he leapt off the mountain, he was able to breathe. As he continued circling, Hughe quickly reminded Iggi why they took such a risk and told him to look around as he concentrated on flying.

"I know that, you big iguana, don't be such a grump," Iggi said.

Hughe felt the best course of action would be to fly straight ahead and changed his direction, once he was certain that his wings had adjusted sufficiently. Hughe continued looking forward as he spoke to Iggi, telling him he must be his eyes and to look in every direction. He had to stay focused because, he warned, his wings might not have sufficient strength to continue and so time was of the essence.

"Alright," Iggi said, "What a worry wart!" Don't get your tail in a knot," he said and looked all around.

Iggi first looked to the right and could see nothing more than what they first saw when they came to the island, lots of trees and plants, although these had no fruit. As Hughe flew on, Iggi then looked to the left and saw only sand and rocks. He grumbled,

"I don't see anything special. Maybe there's nothing on this island to see."

I disagree, said Hughe with such abruptness that he made Iggi suspicious.

"What're you saying?" He asked. "What're you not telling us? How come you're certain something is here, when I keep telling you there isn't?"

Hughe did not want to lie, especially to a friend, and felt the best thing to do was to be honest. He quickly explained to Iggi,

Something is tugging in my mind. I felt it when we first came to the island. I hoped it was our lost friends, Sandy and Tuff. But I dismissed that thought quickly because it came from the direction of the island. My telepathy at this stage in my life is unpredictable and fallible. Only with continued exercise will my talents become more reliable. In due course, as I age, I will be able to depend on them, but right now they are uncertain.

Iggi became irate and told the dragon,

"So you thought it was best to lie to us."

No, Hughe replied. *I simply did not want to give you false hope.*

"So you lied." Hughe could sense the hurt in Iggi's words because of the rapport they shared. Hughe's words lost credibility because he realized a lie was a lie, no matter what good intentions there were and sadly admitted,

Yes, I lied, and his eyes became watery. Iggi's hurt was great and he was not going to let Hughe off easily.

"You're not only telepathic, you're also telepathetic," he said, and it was Hughe who was at a loss for words as they continued their mission in eerie silence.

Chapter 12:

NOW YOU SEE ME

C al and Hope sat impatiently fumbling to eat the remaining fruit but neither was really hungry. Hope offered Cal the newly cut slices, but the centaur-boy simply shook his head. Hope understood; as hard as she tried, she could not get any of the pieces close to her mouth before she placed them back in the knapsack. Though neither expressed their concerns, both of them knew that each was worried about their companions, for it had been over an hour since they departed. High above the mountain ridge they had loomed, until both passed over the mountain and were lost to sight. As if reading her thoughts, which he could not, Cal asked Hope if she thought they were alright.

"I do not know," she replied, and Cal noticed sadness in her eyes. "But I'm thinking maybe we should look for them in case they are in trouble."

"I agree," said Cal quickly, "But if we are to do that it would be best to do it soon before it gets dark!"

Hope nodded in agreement and started to pick up the rinds from what little fruit they had eaten, while Cal dug a hole with his hooves to bury them. Hope placed the fruits they had left untouched in the knapsack Iggi had brought with him. Hope remembered what her sisters Flora and Fauna had taught her.

"When one takes from the environment, make sure it is no more than necessary. That way the environment has time to grow back what it has lost."

Hope was always careful to remember that fact, for she had spent many years in the comfort of her island and had great respect for its beauty and knew it was everyone's responsibility to keep it beautiful. As Cal and Hope had finished gathering the remaining rinds to bury, they were about to leave when high above them they heard whooping and hollering. It was Iggi, waving one hand in a circle as he held on tight to Hughe with the other. The multi-colored dragon continued his slow descent, gliding in circles lower and lower, while Iggi kept yelling that they would not believe what they had found. Hughe was only a few feet from the ground when Iggi jumped off him unexpectedly and fell on his rear.

"Are you alright?" Asked Cal.

"Of course I'm alright," Iggi said, dusting himself off. "In fact, we're all okay," he said smiling.

"What are you talking about?" Asked Hope. "Did you find Sandy and Tuff?"

Iggi's eyes were sad as his excitement faded and he simply replied, "No."

Hughe, seeing that the fairy was too choked up to continue, replied,

That would indeed be wonderful news, but what we found was only good news.

Cal and Hope wished they had found their lost friends, but Cal asked bravely what it was they had found. Hughe replied,

It was a house, of enormous size. He added, seeing the fairy-boy off to the side, *it is possible that Sandy and Tuff made it to the safety of this island.*

Iggi's eyes lit up upon hearing this and he told everyone that if they were there, they had better hurry up and get there before dark.

"A house? Whose house?" Hope asked.

I do not know, answered Hughe, *as we were unable to land. We only saw that it indeed was a house.*

Hope grew alarmed at hearing what the dragon was saying. If it indeed was a house, as Hughe and Iggi were certain it was, then who or what was living there? Another thought crossed Hope's mind as she wondered if it was friend or foe and would it be hostile toward unwanted guests? Hope was certain that the only way they would know for sure was to go to the house. Hughe, sensing the fear in Hope's thoughts, suggested it might be best if they allowed him to go first.

Few things exist that will bravely challenge a dragon, even a young one, he said. *I will do my best to protect you in case of a sudden attack. That way all of you could get away quickly.*

Hughe had never had friends before, choosing to remain a loner because he was different from the rest of the dragons. How quickly things change, he thought, for the old Hughe seemed like a distant memory now that he had friends he cared about and who in return cared about him. Though they were human (well, more so than he was), they understood what he was feeling and going through because they themselves were in similar situations. Hughe knew the only thing he could do was to protect his new-found friends, even if at great risk to him and his mission. Hope, who was still in rapport with Hughe, rubbed the dragon's head and told him,

"We would do no less for you, because you are part of our family."

Cal and Iggi scrambled to gather their belongings as Hope looked at Hughe, who seemed worried.

"Is something wrong?" She asked. Hughe simply replied,

We shall soon see, but we should not get our hopes up too high in case we are let down by what we discover.

Hope simply replied,

"But it is possible, and as long as there is the slightest chance of finding them, we have to take the risk."

I agree, said Hughe, and off they went over the mountain.

Cal led the group up the treacherous terrain with Iggi close behind, while Hope and Hughe brought up the rear. Cal was sure-footed on the mountainous range because centaurs were quite adept at climbing, and were almost as skillful as dragons.

He is quite good, Hughe remarked, admiring the young centaur-boy's grace and speed.

"Yes," Hope replied. "I understand their hooves are sensitive enough to determine where and if they can safely climb. He is confident enough to tell us when and where to step. I am certainly glad he is concentrating on what he can do and not on what he cannot do."

Cal and Iggi made it to the top of the mountain and Iggi yelled,

"There it is, and I told you it was a house."

Cal and Iggi waited for the others to arrive at their vantage point. As they looked where the fairy was pointing, they were awestruck by what they saw. At the base of the mountain, a glass house loomed. It was surrounded by a vegetable garden as well as fruit and nut trees of every variety. Iggi could not contain his excitement or his hunger as he raced down the mountainside and slid half way down. Cal just shook his head in disbelief and said,

"Is that all he ever thinks about? Food?" And he galloped down to where the fairy was already gathering fruit and nuts. Cal noticed that the various trees were smaller than those they had encountered earlier but no less laden with fruit. Cal asked Iggi if he was going to eat all of it by himself and Iggi replied,

"Just be quiet and help me pick some vegetables."

While Iggi and Cal continued picking a variety of fruits, nuts and vegetables, Hope asked Hughe if maybe they should knock on the door to see if anyone was home. As they walked to the entrance to the enormous glass house, Iggi and Cal could be heard yelling at each other as they gathered their bounty of food.

"That is enough food," said Cal, "My arms are full."

"It's not your arms I want to load. Now turn around so I can put some more on your back."

"I am a centaur, not some pack-mule you can overload," Cal retorted angrily.

Hope and Hughe just shook their heads as they continued to the great door. Hope grasped the door knocker and rapped three times. The glass knocker was so loud it reverberated throughout the house and Hope thought it would crack. Hope and Hughe waited for someone or something to answer the door and after a few moments knocked again. Hughe touched Hope and said,

It would appear that the house is uninhabited, at least for the moment. Might we try another approach? He asked.

"What do you suggest?" Asked Hope, but she knew already what he was going to say.

The simplest approach is always the best. It could be that our host, not expecting any visitors, might have felt it was safe to leave the door unlocked.

Hope was apprehensive, but Hughe assured her he would be right by her side as she turned the knob and heard a click. The door swung open as the muse peered in and said gently,

"Hello, is anyone here?"

When no one answered, Hughe nudged her with his snout to enter the dwelling and was surprised by what they saw. Because it was made of glass, parts of the house shone where the sun's rays came through, illuminating their surroundings. Hope and Hughe entered the glass structure and noticed that everything in it was also made of glass. There were huge columns at the main entrance to the room as they walked in and they could see large pieces of glass furniture and tables carved into place.

"It is beautiful," breathed Hope and the dragon could not have agreed with her more.

The strange house was multi-leveled and the rooms seemed endless as the natural light from the sun shone through, casting its warmth upon the house. The translucent house created a cascade of color wherever the sun shone on it. Hughe commented on the size of the house, saying that although it would surely not be comfortable for an average dragon, that it would fit him and his companions perfectly. As Hope continued to be awed by the way the light seemed to dance off the furniture, she noticed her companion, who was walking to where the brightest of the lights shone on his multi-colored scales. Brighter and brighter he glowed until it seemed to Hope that he started to glimmer and then fade away slowly. Panic flooded through her as she stared at the spot where the dragon had just been; he had simply vanished.

"Hughe," cried Hope. "Where are you?"

Hope ran to where she knew Hughe was a moment before and bumped into something large. As she groped around, she grabbed what could only be his tail.

"Hughe, is that you?" She asked nervously.

Hughe was puzzled by the sound of panic in the muse's voice and assured her,

Yes, it is I. Why did you cry out that way?

Hope asked Hughe if he could see her and the dragon told her he could but wanted to know what was wrong.

I am right in front of you, he said. *Do you not see me?* He asked.

Hope, her outstretched hands grasping what looked like air, replied that she could not see him because he simply was not there. Hope, seeking desperately for an answer, asked Hughe again if he could see her. Hughe knew for certain the muse did not play games, so something must be very wrong. He repeated that he could see her very clearly. Hope explained to Hughe what she had seen or rather had not seen, about the way the light danced strangely off his scales when he came into contact with it, how it seemed to waver around him like shimmering water and then he was gone.

Hmm, said Hughe, *and you say it was when the light shone off my scales that I started to disappear? Have you seen this before?* He asked.

"Yes," she said excitedly, and explained that she had first seen it happen when he and Iggi were scaling the mountain; he was there one minute and gone the next. She continued to explain how Iggi seemed to hover, like he was floating on air, but she knew that was impossible and assumed she was tired from the day's journey.

"I am certain Cal must have seen this happen. He was watching you both as well."

Hughe shook his head, although Hope could not see him and said,

That was why he seemed so determined to lead the way up and down the mountain.

"I do not understand," said Hope.

Hughe explained.

Young Cal is considered unfit by centaur standards because of the human defect he suffers. Cal indeed must have seen what you did and when he saw me apparently disappear, he thought his condition was getting worse.

"Oh, poor Cal," said Hope.

I want to try something, Hope, but you will have to release my tail. We will lose contact for only a moment.

"What are you going to do?" She asked nervously.

I am going to reappear if all goes well. At least I will attempt to by moving out of the sunlight.

Hope released the dragon's tail and immediately lost contact with him, but she was certain he was still there. She heard shuffling and assumed that Hughe was moving. Suddenly she saw a strange glimmer of light, small at first but becoming larger. First Hope saw Hughe's snout appearing as if out of thin air. It was only when she continued to watch that she saw a head start to appear and slowly the glimmer started to form a body until Hughe finally reappeared whole and intact.

"You did it!" Exclaimed Hope as she rushed to where Hughe was and rubbed the dragon's body.

I can only take your word for it, because to me I did nothing more than simply move out of the light.

Hope pondered this and asked Hughe if any dragon he had ever known had done a miraculous thing like this before. Hughe shook his head and replied,

dragons are extremely large, thus making their presence hard to mask, so I do not think this is possible.

Yet, for all his doubt, he could not come up with a reason why he was able to do such a thing.

"You told us," said Hope, "That dragons usually come in a variety of solid colors and, as far as you knew, your multi-colored scales are quite unique."

Yes, that is true, but I do not understand what you are trying to say, he replied.

"I will explain as best I can," she said, and asked him if he had ever heard of genetics.

No, I am afraid I have not, he said.

"Well, every creature, whether plant or animal, is comprised of many different genes passed down from generation to generation. Though the species share similar qualities, such as form, each has differences that set them apart from one another. In the case of gods and humans, we share the same physical traits, but it is our own genetic makeup that gives us our individual differences. The gods are gifted with immortality, which sets us apart from humans. Dragons are gifted with a variety of talents, such as fire-breathing, flying, telepathy and so on, yet you derive from the reptile species, sharing the same looks, but differing in size, strength and talents."

Hughe shook his head once again. This was all so complicated, but he was beginning to understand. Hope was glad she had paid attention in science class and continued to explain to Hughe.

"As each new generation comes into existence, they share traits passed on from long ago; these are called recessive genes. It is these genes that come randomly into existence from an ancestor or ancestors that make us what we are today. I suspect that a relative of yours somewhere along your line had the ability to camouflage itself as a way to defend itself from predators."

Hughe's ears perked up when she said this and he replied that he understood.

So, you are saying that my relatives who were reptiles, being smaller in size and unable to breathe fire or fly, had to adapt as well as they could, and some of them could hide in such a way.

Hope nodded in agreement and was glad he understood what she was trying to explain to him.

"Yes," she said. "Some may have had one form of ability or the other, but not all of them. Only through evolution did the dragons, a sub-species of the original reptiles, gain a variety of talents. My sister Fauna, the muse of animal husbandry, told me once of a lizard called a chameleon that could blend in with its background as a defense."

Hope quickly explained that it could not disappear like Hughe did, which indicated his recessive gene had developed differently in the dragon species.

This is unbelievable, said Hughe, *as well as wonderful.*

"It all makes sense now," she said, "Why when we first ran into you, Iggi did not see you hiding in the bushes. You must have blended in so perfectly he assumed it was safe. The same thing happened when you seemed to disappear while Cal and I were watching you on the cliff."

Hope felt the excitement he was feeling and was overjoyed by his new sense of worth.

Like my other abilities, Hughe said, *it seems to come and go. Maybe with experience it might just prove worthwhile.*

Hope agreed and suggested they explore his new possibilities, but for now, as the place seemed uninhabited, they might want to rest here for the night.

Agreed, he said, just as Iggi and Cal burst into the house carrying supplies.

"Where are you?" Iggi called, as they saw Cal fumbling with the food, trying not to drop it.

"So," said Iggi, while Cal placed the food on the table, "Is anyone here?"

"No," replied Hope, "The place is deserted."

"Great, then we can rest up for the night and have a feast fit for a king."

They went to the kitchen, where all of the plates and utensils were strangely large, and after an hour of preparing all that Cal and Iggi had found, they sat down for their evening meal while Hope explained what they had discovered about Hughe's hidden talent.

"So Hughe has the ability to disappear," exclaimed Cal, "That is incredible!"

Iggi was too busy eating to take part in the conversation, as he kept asking Cal to pass the fruit his way.

"Not to disappear entirely," said Hope, "But actually to blend in with his surroundings so perfectly..."

Hope was about to explain more when Iggi asked her to pass the vegetables on her side of the table. The fairy had, during the course of everyone's conversation, piled incredible amounts of food on his plate, so much so that his head could hardly be seen.

"I am glad to hear it had nothing to do with my defect. I was afraid it was getting worse," said Cal.

"I thought maybe I was starting to see things, too, but I was afraid to mention anything," Hope said.

"You said Hope that Iggi did not disappear when Hughe did. That means there may be limits to his ability."

"Or," said Hope, "Like his other talents, this ability may grow once he has gained experience. Right now, it seems to happen when he is least expecting it, like when he is in direct sun, but maybe in time he will be able to store the sun's rays and use this ability to his and our advantage."

Hughe nodded in agreement, speaking through Hope.

How truly wonderful and unique it is for my kin, and how beneficial it might prove in scouting enemy territory in case of war.

"Dragons have war?" Asked Cal.

Yes and no, he said. *Dragons challenge each other for territory, thus gaining status among each other, which is why my parents are held in high regard. They were wise enough to realize that if they combined their efforts, they would be dominant, and then, eventually, they fell in love.*

"That is so sweet," said Hope.

"Yeah, yeah, very romantic," said Iggi, as he was stuffing his face with food. "Now, if no one else is hungry, just pass it down my way." His wings buzzed in agreement.

Cal just shook his head as Hope and Hughe laughed. As they finished dinner and cleared away the food, Hope assigned rooms to the others. Hughe, because of his size would sleep downstairs in front of the fireplace. This was his choice because he needed the warmth. Also, in case the owner returned unexpectedly, he or she would think twice about approaching a sleeping dragon. Iggi had chosen a room with pillows of various sizes strewn about the floor, while Cal preferred an empty room because centaurs slept standing up. Instead of saying goodnight, Iggi made a snide comment that when they got back to Cal's island, how fun it would be to go centaur tipping, a remark that Cal did not appreciate. Hope, having made certain the others were quite comfortable, chose a normal looking room that resembled one for humans. It had an enormous bed, whose mattress was stuffed with some kind of feathers. The moment her head touched the equally stuffed pillows, she fell fast asleep.

Chapter 13:

ENIGMA

Morning came and Hope woke up to the sun's rays split into prisms throughout the room. She admired the way they beamed off the glass furniture, creating a splendor of rainbow color. Hope rose quietly so as not to disturb the others in case they were still sleeping. Opening the door to her room, she made her way back to the living room. She was startled by how clean everything was, as if they had just arrived. The dishes were all washed and put away in the kitchen. Hope had wanted to do them the night before but decided they could sit till morning. Now, here they were, clean. How nice, thought Hope, one of the boys must have cleaned up before he went to bed. No matter how much they disagreed with each other, everyone contributed. As usual, Iggi and Cal could be heard arguing as they made their way into the main room.

Cal: "You snore."

Iggi: "I don't either."

Cal: "Oh yes you do!" It sounded like a herd of wild beasts.

Iggi: "You should know, horse-fly, being part mule."

Cal: "Coming from someone who looks like he should be guarding a bridge, I think I am way ahead on the evolutionary scale."

Iggi grumbled, Cal stomped his hooves, when Hope, looking for some way to end their bickering, called that breakfast was ready. Iggi sat next to Hughe, while Hope sat next to the centaur-boy on the other end, hoping that by separating them they would calm down. Hughe sat silently watching the two boys stare at each other across the table as they ate the fruits, nuts and vegetables they had harvested off the trees the night before. As they finished eating in silence, Cal offered to help Hope clear the table but she declined his offer, saying she would do it since he had cleared last night's dishes. A puzzled look came across the centaur-boy's face as he replied,

"I do not understand what you are saying."

Hope replied,

"Last night when we had finished eating I was going to clean the dishes, but was tired and left them to do in the morning. When I got up to do them, I noticed they had been cleaned and put away."

Cal shook his head,

"I did not do them. Gargoyle-boy probably did."

Iggi became irate at hearing what Cal had called him and said loudly,

"I'm not a gargoyle. I'm a fairy and I didn't do them either. I was too busy snoring according to the talking mule."

Hughe's ears perked up and, sensing that he wanted to communicate, Hope gently placed her hand on him.

I distinctly heard someone shuffling about in the kitchen as they were doing dishes and heard them humming a tune. Are you sure that neither of you did them?

"First off, I don't sing," said Iggi adamantly, "And second, I don't do dishes. That's a woman's job."

Iggi, looking across the room, saw that his words had hurt Hope and apologized quickly, then continued,

"I mean it's true. I didn't do them."

Everyone looked at each other in amazement as Hughe asked,

Then who did?

"I did." A voice came out of nowhere.

Iggi: "I thought you didn't do them," looking suspiciously at Cal.

Cal: "I did not say anything. Besides, I already told you I was tired and fell fast asleep."

Iggi: "Maybe you sleepwalked."

Cal: "Centaurs do no such thing. That is a human trait. How about you? Maybe you long to be a domestic goddess in your sleep," he smirked.

Iggi: "Take that back."

Cal: "I will not. You take it back."

Hope interrupted their bickering and asked if either of them had said they did the dishes. Both boys shook their heads in a rare moment of agreement.

I distinctly heard someone say that they had done them, said Hughe and asked Hope if she had spoken.

Hope also shook her head and said she was too busy refereeing the argument between the boys.

If no one did the dishes and none of us spoke, then who did? He asked.

"I did!" Said a voice out of thin air as everyone stared at each other in amazement.

"Ghosts," said Iggi, shuddering.

"There are no such things as ghosts." said Cal. "Centaurs believe in only what they can see."

Hughe and Hope both knew the centaur-boy was incorrect, for throughout history, cases had been reported and just because something could not be seen did not mean it did not exist. There were more important questions to be asked, however, and it was neither the time nor the place to challenge Cal's false assumptions. Hughe reached out with his mind and felt a tug much stronger than before; there was no doubt that they were not alone in the house. As the others sat patiently, Hughe focused on the immediate surroundings and with a slight push, was able to pinpoint the unseen voice's whereabouts.

There, he said, and with lightning speed and agility, quickly pounced toward the unsuspecting presence. The others were taken aback by the dragon's movements and noticed that he was staring toward one corner of the room.

"What is it?" Asked Hope anxiously as she followed Hughe and touched his back.

We are not alone, he said, *and though we cannot see it, I have got whatever it is cornered. I suggest we ask it who and what it wants with us,* he said.

Hughe and the others could not see the ghost, but if the dragon said there was someone there, then it was true. Hope continued towards where Hughe had said it was, although she felt foolish asking the air if anyone was there and what it was doing in the house. The air was silent, unlike before, but then suddenly a soft, gentle voice was heard.

"Please do not hurt me. I mean you no harm. My name is Enigma and this is my home. I am a giantess, though one could not tell by my appearance."

The others were shocked: a giantess; that would explain why everything was bigger than normal. Why the trees bearing fruits and nuts were plentiful and the garden so well-tended, but why were they unable to see her. Hope asked if Enigma had been here all along and the voice admitted she had been, but was afraid they had meant to harm her and so chose to remain silent until she could be sure whether they were friend or foe.

Hughe, convinced that she meant them no harm, backed away from the unseen giantess so as not to make her feel defensive.

"If you have nothing to hide and mean us no harm, why don't you show yourself so we can see you?" Asked Iggi suspiciously.

Enigma was silent for a moment and they thought at first that she had gone, but then they heard her sad voice explain that, as much as she would like that, she could not do as they asked.

"Just what I thought," said Iggi. "You're nothing but a lot of hot air. Maybe we should let our pet dragon eat you for breakfast."

Hughe was not going to do any such thing, but she did not know that dragons do not eat people and furthermore, that they were nobody's pets. The unseen giantess gasped and begged them to allow her to explain. It was not that she did not want to appear, but that she could not because she was an invisible giantess. She also explained that, although she was seven feet tall, she was smaller than other giants.

"For some reason, when I was thirteen, I became invisible."

"Are you ugly?" Asked Iggi.

Cal gave him a little kick, while the others glared at Iggi, who had learned early on that it was best to apologize for his rudeness, even though he was simply asking a question. Enigma was silent once again and then spoke suddenly,

"I do not consider myself ugly, but I suppose beauty is in the eye of the beholder, and there is no one to behold me," she sighed mournfully.

Hope said reassuringly, "I am certain you are as beautiful on the outside as you seem to be on the inside."

Hughe and Cal offered their assurances as well. Even Iggi chimed in, "Yeah, what they said."

Although Enigma could not be seen, nevertheless she could be heard and the little encouragement they offered her seemed to brighten her disposition. As the four were curious about Enigma, she was equally curious about them.

"What brought you here to the island," asked Enigma, "And how long are you planning to stay?"

Enigma told them that it had been a long time since she had visitors and she welcomed the opportunity for conversation. The other giants were very polite to her, never rude, but like most people, they found it unnerving to talk to someone they could not see. Enigma suggested that they exchange stories as she prepared breakfast. She apologized for not having more varieties of food, but said that she had not expected any guests.

"That is alright," said Hope, and offered to help her pick the fruits and vegetables in the garden. When they sat down for breakfast, Hope explained everything that had happened to them so far and why it was so important to find their destinies. Enigma listened with great enthusiasm as she in turn explained her story and how she wished she could join them on their quest.

"I am very sorry about your friends," Enigma continued, "But they are not here on the island. Maybe they have gone to a different one."

"You mean there are other islands?" Asked Cal.

"Oh yes," Enigma replied, "But each one is different. The current is strong and could have carried them safely to another store, but which one I do not know."

Hope thanked her for her words of encouragement and her hospitality and asked if there was anything they could do in return. Enigma sighed; no one had ever cared enough to ask about her problem; people just assumed she did not want to talk about it. She explained that it was lonely not having anyone to talk to who would understand and she was grateful that they were willing to listen to her.

Hughe, who had remained silent up till now, brushed up against the muse and suggested,

Maybe we could take her along. Surely the boat could magically adapt to her size, as it was able to adapt to mine.

"Hughe, I could kiss you!" She exclaimed loudly, as the others looked at her in shock. "I mean, that is a wonderful idea." She said, blushing.

Hope quickly explained what Hughe had suggested and the others agreed, even Iggi, who normally did not like people. Enigma was astounded. Here were four strangers who did not owe her anything, willing to help her with her problem. This was too much for the giantess to absorb and she started to cry. Iggi started to grumble at hearing Enigma cry and reached into his knapsack, grabbed a towel and held it up in the air. Everyone was astonished by Iggi's compassion. The others watched as the towel seemed to float in the air, but in reality, the giantess was simply taking the towel in her hand in order to wipe her eyes.

"Thank you," she said to Iggi, who simply replied that he didn't want to drown in tears and then grumbled,

"You're welcome," hoping that no one else heard. "What?" He said, catching Cal staring at him.

"Nothing," said the centaur-boy. "I thought I heard something but I must have been imagining it."

"Whatever, push-cart pony," Iggi replied.

The giantess laughed, which seemed to echo through the glass house. Hope herself found it hard to keep from smiling. Hughe suggested,

Perhaps it might be easier to define her presence, Enigma, if you had some way of making yourself visible to us.

Enigma replied,

"I have thought of that, but anything I wear disappears on my body."

"That makes sense," said Hope, whose clothes were opaque as well.

Iggi smirked, "That's if she *is* wearing clothes."

"Of course I am!" Said Enigma. "What kind of giantess do you think I am?" She replied as she picked up Iggi in her unseen hand.

"I was just asking," he said, as his legs dangled in the air. "Now put me down," he demanded.

The invisible giantess did as he asked and apologized for her temper.

"That is okay," said Hope, as she watched Iggi being put back down. "He likes to shock people. It is best to just ignore him." She shot Iggi another look.

Suddenly, Enigma began to sob again.

"It is no use; I am destined to remain invisible forever."

"Maybe not," said Cal thinking with his superior intelligence.

"Do you have an idea?" Asked Hope.

"I do," he said rather proudly, "But it may take me a few minutes to think it out."

Hope, Hughe, Iggi, and especially Enigma, sat silently as the centaur-boy ran different scenarios through his mind.

"Hope, when we first saw Hughe disappear, only he disappeared, correct?"

Hope nodded and replied that it looked like Iggi was floating.

"Right, Iggi did not disappear, only Hughe. Maybe it is the same principle that an object has to be a part of him, or her in this case, and so is not affected by their ability."

Interesting, said Hughe, brushing up against the centaur-boy, *and your reasoning is that he was foreign matter, unnatural, and so was unaffected.*

"Hey!" Yelled Iggi. "I heard that and it's not nice."

"No offense," said Cal, obviously enjoying the unexpected jab at Iggi.

"Exactly! Enigma's use of clothes is natural, but when she picked up the towel or even Iggi, they remained visible. I see what you are getting at," said Hope. "It must only affect their immediate person, but what about the house? It is also transparent."

Cal said, "I suspect it was built that way. As Enigma cannot be seen, what better place to live in than a transparent house: no need for modesty."

"Yes, that is correct," said Enigma. "The other giants built this house so that I may live in privacy with my predicament. Their concern was for my safety, as well as theirs, in not being able to see me. They were afraid that they might step on me or worse, trip over me and hurt themselves. They were very considerate toward my feelings in being unique."

"That's all well and great," said Iggi, "But how does that help her?" He asked.

"I was thinking," said Cal, "That if maybe she wore a flower, it might make her easier to see. Certainly there are plenty of them growing in the garden."

"Doesn't that put us back in the same hole?" Asked Iggi. "Wouldn't the flower disappear as well?"

"No," said Hope catching on. "The flower is natural to the environment, but unnatural to her and that means she can be seen."

"Huh?" Said Iggi, scratching his head. Hope tried to explain in terms that Iggi could understand.

"Hughe's scales, when in direct sunlight, give him the ability to blend in because that is natural to him, but when something unnatural *to him*, like you, rode him as he climbed the ridge, you remained visible because you were unnatural."

"If one more person calls me unnatural I'm going to scream. Oh great, now you've done it. I have a giant headache, no pun intended," he said.

"Never mind, Iggi, we will show you," Cal said, and asked Enigma if she could retrieve a flower from the garden.

The giantess excused herself as the others made a pathway, hoping she could fit among them as they heard thunderous footsteps as she passed them. In just a moment's time, the door through which they had entered seemed to open miraculously as she made her way outside. As they waited patiently, the giantess could be heard humming in her excitement as she made her way back inside from the garden. She carried a very visible red rose.

"Is that you, Enigma?" Asked Cal.

"Of course it is, silly!" She said. "Unless there is another giant who can turn invisible," Enigma replied. "Oh look, there he is, right by Iggi."

The fairy jumped so high he fell off the chair he was sitting on.

"Just kidding," said Enigma, giggling.

"Real funny, spooky," he said. "Isn't there a house you could haunt?" He grumbled. "Oh never mind. Now that she has the flower, what're you going to do with it?" He asked Cal.

"I am thinking that if she placed it on her head, she would be more visible. At least we would be able to tell where she is at any moment."

"And if it doesn't work," said Iggi, "Then what?"

"I would be no worse off than before," she said sadly. "That is what you meant, is it not?" She asked Cal.

"Yes," he said, "But I am certain that it will, if it follows my reasoning."

Enigma let out a big sigh, "Well, it is a chance I am willing to take," and she asked what she was to do with the flower. "I cannot carry it around with me forever," she said.

"No, of course not," Cal replied. "I want you to wear it in your hair."

"Her hair?" Asked Iggi. "But why?"

"Boys," said Hope. "Because a girl likes to put ribbons in her hair, even a giantess."

"Exactly," said Cal. "My sister and her friends liked to do their hair in a pony-tail with barrettes of all colors. They felt it made them more attractive," he said.

The giantess asked, "You think I am attractive?"

Cal, taken by surprise, looked down at the ground shyly, shuffling his hooves to and fro and said,

"Certainly there is more to you than meets the eye," and blushed.

"That is very sweet," said Enigma. "No boy has ever called me beautiful."

"I did not say you were beautiful," he stammered.

"Oh," said the giantess sadly, "I just assumed you were complimenting me."

Sensing that his words had hurt Enigma, Cal explained quickly that he meant it is not what a person looks like on the outside, but what a person is on the inside that counts.

"Oh," she said as her voice brightened, "The same goes for you."

Cal was again caught off-guard and simply replied,

"Thank you."

Iggi interrupted.

"If you two love birds are through, can we just get on with it?"

"By all means," said Enigma, as she placed the flower in her hair. Waiting patiently for the flower to disappear, they were pleased after a few moments' time when it did no such thing and remained visible.

"How does it look?" She asked. "Did it disappear?"

Hope replied, "No, it is still there and it is quite beautiful. This is just a temporary solution," she said" Until we can figure out a way to make it more permanent."

"May I look?" Enigma asked.

"*You* can see yourself?" Hope asked.

"Oh yes," she replied. "How else would I know when my hair needed brushing or my clothes needed washing?"

That seems to make sense, said Hughe, touching Cal. *As for why the flower did not disappear, it is a living thing, although temporary, and thus is unnatural to her. The clothes she wears are natural to her, so they remain invisible.*

"Here we go again," said Iggi. "Oh, my head! Let me get this straight. So the pestle with the vessel is the brew that is true?"

This time it was the others who said in unison, "Huh?"

"Never mind," he said. "It's something I heard once. Does this mean we can go now?" He asked.

"Yes, we can go as soon as Enigma is ready," Cal said.

"Let me just grab some things," she said, as the flower danced around the house.

"Okay, and we will just take along some food from your garden for the journey," Cal said. He was about to ask Iggi for help, but the fairy was already outside.

"Typical," muttered Cal and followed to where Iggi had gone.

"Do you need help?" Hope asked Enigma.

"No, thank you," replied Enigma, "I am almost done packing some clothes."

The dragon touched Hope, who replied, "Hughe says he has been meaning to talk to Iggi about that."

"What?" He asked, having returned with an armful of food. "Do I smell?" And Iggi bent down and sniffed his clothes. "I don't smell anything."

"The point is, *we* do," said Cal and smiled.

"Whatever," Iggi grumbled.

Enigma came out of the room where she had been packing, which was evident by the rose that appeared to be floating, but was not.

"I am ready," she said.

Hope smiled at Enigma, who may have smiled back, but the muse just had to assume she did.

"Good," said Cal. "The sooner we leave, the sooner we are able to accomplish what we need to do."

Hope noticed the way Cal had looked at the giantess, and although he could not see her, Hope sensed that there was something special between them. Iggi grabbed as much food as he could for the adventure while Cal just shook his head. Soon, they departed the glass house and made their way to the swan boat, which was waiting for them patiently.

Chapter 14:

DEARLY DEPARTED

W hen they arrived at the swan boat, it looked at them and seeing the floating rose, seemed distressed. Hughe noticed the strange way the boat was eyeing the rose, as if tracking its movement. As Iggi prepared to board, with Hope following, the boat continued to eye the approaching rose. Cal and Hughe remained behind while they allowed Enigma to go on first. The moment the giantess approached the swan boat it acted strangely, started to honk, as if panicked by the intrusion, and lowered its wings to block Enigma from boarding. Much to the surprise of the others, try as she might, the boat would not let Enigma climb on, but just continued its distress call. Time and again the giantess tried to board, but the swan boat would not let her pass. Hope tried to calm the boat but it ignored her attempts and continued its incessant honking. The boat made such a racket, the others had to cover their ears to drown out the sound.

"What's up with quackers?" Iggi asked.

"I do not know," said Hope. "For some reason, it seems panicked." Hope could not calm the boat, despite her best efforts.

Hughe, observing the boat's behavior, said,

It seems the boat does not want Enigma to board.

"Why, asked Cal?"

I do not know, said Hughe, *but if we are to continue we must find out the reason. Certainly there is something more here than meets the eye.*

"What do you mean, It won't let her on?" Demanded Iggi.

"Maybe it does not like me," said Enigma mournfully.

"That is impossible," said Cal. "We like you, so therefore, the boat has to like you."

"You do?" Asked Enigma. "You are so sweet to say that." Cal blushed at hearing her remark; no centaur-filly had ever said such a thing to him. Iggi heard the exchange and interrupted,

"If you two are finished, maybe we can figure out why it won't let you on," he said.

Cal blushed again, as surely as Enigma must have, but fortunately she could not be seen.

"Hmm, this is indeed strange," said Hope. "The boat has never acted this way before."

"Maybe it is sick," said Cal.

Hope shook her head and said she did not think so; even though the boat was magically animated, it was not really alive, and so could not get sick.

"Then why will it not allow me on?" Asked Enigma.

"I am uncertain," said Hope, "But we will find out."

"I'll find out," Iggi said, and marched up to the boat, demanding to know why it refused to let the giantess on.

"Listen here, you overgrown chicken, if you don't let her on I'm going to pluck your feathers one by one and let the dragon pick his teeth with them after he has eaten you. Now let her on," he demanded, his wings buzzing angrily.

Hughe, who normally would not threaten anyone, licked his teeth for added effect. The swan boat craned its neck at Iggi, surprised by his threatening manner and stared blankly at him.

"Well, what's it going to be?" He demanded with his hands on his waist. "Do I call the dragon for din-din, or do you let her on?"

The swan boat continued to stare down the fairy, while Iggi stared back. Who was going to back down? The swan boat stared at the fairy, as if wondering why he would threaten it so, and finally relinquished its position, raising its wings so the others could get on.

"See," Iggi said triumphantly, "Nothing to it. My mouth is good for something besides eating." Iggi continued to march confidently as he made his way to Hughe, Enigma and Cal and told them, "All aboard."

The boys allowed Enigma to go ahead of them as she made her way to where the boat was, but the moment she tried to get on again the swan boat honked in panic and blocked her entry.

"Oh no," said Cal fearfully. "Here we go again." As the others watched, amazed by the boat's behavior, Hughe brushed up against Iggi,

who was closest to him.

"What?" Asked Iggi, ready to pounce on the boat again. "Quit shoving."

I did not mean to shove you, said Hughe, *only to make contact. Maybe we are looking at this all wrong,* Hughe said. *Maybe it is not that the boat does not want to let Enigma on but more likely that it is unable to,* Hughe suggested.

"Are you crazy, basilisk-breath?" Iggi said. "This boat has an attitude and I'm the one to adjust it," he said as he was about to give the boat another round of yelling.

Please, said Hughe, *relay what I have said to Hope.*

Iggi reluctantly did as Hughe requested and Hope said it was possible. Hope explained to Enigma that the boat's magic took Hope to where she was needed most. Enigma understood.

"So that means you do not have to take me," she said sadly.

On hearing this, Cal became equally sad.

"I still say we should let the dragon eat it," said Iggi stubbornly. "I mean, this place isn't so bad."

Cal readily agreed. "It is not like there is a place for me in the centaur village. My near-sightedness would only remind them of their human heritage. Who would want a near-sighted centaur-boy living with them?" He asked sadly.

"I would," said Enigma abruptly. "What better companion for an invisible giantess, than someone who is near-sighted? You would not judge me for my looks, but for my words. Women appreciate men who do not base their friendship on how they appear on the outside but for what is on the inside, as you said," she finished.

Cal remembered how his sister reacted toward the other centaur-colts; she was bored with the way they liked to show off for fillies whom they thought were pretty.

"Boys are so immature," she had told him. Cal normally ignored his sister when she said things like this, but Enigma made him think that perhaps she was right after all. Maybe if he returned to his village he would start to listen to her more often. Cal told the others that his mind was made up, that if the boat would not allow Enigma to ride it, then he was going to stay with her.

"What," said Enigma, surprised? "You would do that for me?"

"No," he said, "For us."

"Are you sure?" Asked Hope.

"Yes, I am," he said firmly.

"Good," said Iggi, "Because I'm tired of hoof-boy sticking his rear in my face," he said, laughing.

"Well, the feeling is mutual, wing-nut," and Cal laughed as well.

Hope, who normally disliked the boys' arguments, surprised herself when she thought how much she would miss their bantering. Hughe suggested,

Maybe this was why the boat would not let Enigma board. It is not her destiny. Maybe we should consult the boat and see if this is the reason for its behavior.

Hope prepared to ask the boat "Yes" and "No" questions, and asked the boat if it would give one honk for "Yes" and two for "No."

After awhile, they learned why the boat reacted the way it did. Hope explained that each one of them had a destiny to fulfill, but for the moment at least, that did not include Enigma.

That makes sense, said Hughe, *the boat brought us to where we were needed most, not realizing that Enigma needed us.*

"Yes," said Hope. "If Cal stays on the island, his problem is temporarily solved."

The future is indeed tricky, Hughe concluded.

"I wish I was able to go with you," said Enigma, "And am sorry that Cal has to stay with me."

"Nothing to be sorry about," exclaimed Cal. "Centaurs prefer the land, not the sea," he chuckled.

"You are all welcome to stay," said Enigma. "The island is big and really quite beautiful."

"I can see it now," exclaimed Iggi. "Some giant will come along and make me a pet. He'll put me in a cage and expect me to sing. You can forget that, ogress, I'm nobody's pet," he said jokingly.

Enigma laughed. "I assure you that would not happen. Most likely they will want to play fairy toss and see who can throw you the farthest."

The others laughed, knowing the giantess was joking, but Iggi was not sure. As much as Hope liked Enigma and her beautiful island, this was not her home. She would greatly miss her sisters, as she was sure they would miss her. Not wanting to offend the giantess, Hope simply explained that it was not her destiny and that she needed to fulfill it, as she hoped to be able to return to her own island.

"I understand," said Enigma, "And I wish you the best on your journey. If you ever come back this way you are certainly welcome on this island."

Hope thanked Enigma and promised that one day she would return and help the giantess solve her problem.

Enigma thanked Hope in kind, saying, "In the short time we have spent together, you have shown great compassion for others, and I am grateful for whatever assistance you may provide in the future. I am certain that if you are truly able to return, you will keep your promise."

Hope thought to herself, what a beautiful person Enigma must be indeed, to forsake her own happiness for others. Truly, she is a giant among giants. Cal and the giantess watched as the others prepared to embark on their journey. Iggi, of course, scrambled to pick as much fruit and vegetables as he could before they left the island. The giantess, seeing him struggling for the larger fruit, picked the ones he could not reach and handed them down to Iggi.

"Thanks," he said as he shoved them into his knapsack.

"You are most welcome, Iggi," she said in her soft voice. Iggi liked the way Enigma spoke to him, never making fun of his size even though he made fun of her. Iggi was not terribly comfortable around people, especially girls, but he appreciated Enigma's gentleness and could see why the centaur-boy liked her. Iggi tried to say something polite, but in his nervousness, the words that came out were,

"You're not bad yourself, even if you're invisible." Then he boarded the boat.

To Cal he added,

"Take care of yourselves, shoe-fly; I won't be around to save your rear."

As the swan boat prepared to leave, closing its wings and looking forward, Hope, Hughe, and Iggi waved good-bye as the centaur-boy waved back and the giantess' rose bobbed up and down. Then the three sailed off into the sea.

Cal apologized to Enigma for what Iggi had said and explained he was always saying the wrong thing. Enigma giggled as she turned to face Cal, which was evident by the way the rose was facing. She said that she thought he was being very sweet.

Puzzled, Cal said, "He was not being sweet. He was being rude to you."

"No, he was not," said Enigma adamantly, "He was complimenting me."

Now the centaur-boy scratched his head in confusion and asked what she meant. Enigma replied that all men had trouble expressing themselves to women they liked and, although Iggi meant to compliment her, it came out all wrong.

"It did?" Asked Cal, shaking his head.

"Yes," said the giantess, "Men lack the ability to express themselves openly and so they go about it in a roundabout way."

Cal used a phrase he had heard often in his journey and replied, "Whatever."

Enigma turned once again to face the boat, which was getting farther away from shore and muttered, "Men!"

Cal also turned to face the boat and replied, "Women," as the others faded from sight on their journey into the new day.

Chapter 15:

SPLASH DOWN

A nd then there were none, Iggi thought to himself. Hughe and
Hope had heard Iggi humming to himself and asked if he was
talking to them.

"Nah, I was just thinking that everywhere we go we either leave
someone or lose someone, and we still haven't figured out why I'm so
big," he said gruffly as his wings started to buzz. "Don't even start with
me," he said.

Hope noticed that Iggi was even more grumpy than usual. The
fairy-boy looked away from the others, choosing to stare back in the
direction from which they had just come. Hope thought that Iggi did
not want to talk, so she retrieved the tome that Clio, the muse of history,
had given her and began to read all that had been recorded.

Hughe, who was resting, opened one eye and then the other.
Sensing that maybe Iggi wanted to talk, he brushed up against the
fairy casually.

"What?" Asked Iggi, surprised by the sudden contact. "No, I don't
miss the rocking horse," Iggi said adamantly. "It's bad enough that I
have to stare at the food stuck between your teeth. I'm glad he's gone
off with the spooky ogress. I'm tired of staring at his best part for days,"
he concluded and shifted away from the dragon suddenly to break the

contact between them. Iggi scooted farther away and continued to stare back toward the island.

Hughe knew that Iggi was hurt by Cal's decision to stay with Enigma, but he refused to let his feelings be known, choosing solitude and anger to mask how he really felt. Sometimes all one has to do is listen to what is not being said in order to find the truth, and Iggi expressed himself all too clearly in his silence. Hope wanted to ask Hughe about their conversation, so she touched him briefly. He explained that Iggi missed Cal and that he just needed time. Hope told Hughe that she understood, and said no more, returning to her perusal of the tome that continued to record their adventures.

The trip was uneventful and the passengers quiet. As the boat continued to paddle, Hope unpacked some fruit for lunch and passed one to each. Iggi, normally so ravenous, sat quietly picking at the fruit Hope handed to him. Day turned to night and they rested while the boat continued sailing toward their unknown destination. When morning came, Hughe and Hope awoke to see Iggi still in the same position as he was the night before. Hope approached Iggi and told him that she missed Cal too.

"Huh?" Said Iggi, his concentration broken by her words. "Oh yeah, I almost forgot about long-ears." Hope, confused by his words, asked Iggi what it was he was staring at then.

"I'm not sure. Probably nothing: I was staring at the waves as we left the island, watching them break against each other," he said.

"What is so unusual about that?" Asked Hope, for she liked to watch them too.

Irritated, Iggi replied, "I told you it's probably nothing, but ever since we left the island a strange wave has been following us," he said.

"Following us?" Hope asked. "How can a wave be following us?"

"I don't know, but it is. I've been watching it since we left and it doesn't crash like the others," he said. "It just keeps moving."

Hope looked where Iggi pointed and at first noticed nothing

unusual; wave after wave seemed to swell and then break: nothing unusual about that, she thought. It was only when Iggi said,

"Look," that the muse actually saw what he was pointing at.

In the middle of the other waves, there seemed to be one that was bubbling and as the others crashed against each other, this one remained the same. Wave after wave crested and crashed down, one on top of the other before repeating the pattern. What Hope noticed was that the middle wave did not change and seemed to be coming directly toward them at high speed.

Hughe, who had also noticed this strange occurrence, watched in amazement with the others as the boat came to a sudden stop. Hope asked the swan boat why it had stopped while the other two continued to stare as the strange wave approached closer. The boat explained in its usual way by honking "Yes" or "No."

"This is where we are needed?" Asked Hope. It honked once "Yes," and then continued to answer her in a series of honks, after which it fell silent, satisfied that it had answered her. Hope explained to Iggi and Hughe why they had stopped so suddenly, but they were too busy to listen, watching instead as the strange wave continued to approach them. Closer and closer it came and then suddenly stopped.

"Where'd it go?" Asked Iggi.

Hughe and Hope looked for the strange wave.

"Maybe it was just our imagination," said Hope, relieved.

"I don't have any imagination," said Iggi. "I know what I saw," he said as his tiny wings buzzed. "You saw it too, oh talentless-one," Iggi continued, as he leaned over the side of the boat and peered into the murky water. As Iggi continued to lean closer to the water, ignoring Hughe's warning, a giant head appeared out of nowhere, staring directly at Iggi.

"Argh," he yelled, and fell off the boat, in his panic grasping for the closest thing he could find. Hughe and Hope finally saw what Iggi had seen and what he was now clutching. As the head rose higher and higher from the ocean depths, a huge, snake-like body with giant wings appeared, its scales as black as night. Its length was indeterminate; there seemed to be no end to the creature.

"Help!" Yelled Iggi. "My imaginations got me," he said, as the creature dove in and out of the water, trying to shake him off.

Hughe and Hope scrambled to help their friend, at a loss what to do as the sea-serpent continued to dive into the water. Between gulps of air, Iggi was yelling for them to help him as the sea-serpent continued to try to shake off its unwelcome rider, slithering through the water while Iggi grasped tighter to its neck.

"Hughe, did you see that?" Hope asked. "The sea-serpent has wings." As he made contact with Hope, Hughe replied that he did.

But it is not a sea-serpent because they do not have wings.

Hope, confused, asked, "Then what is it?" Hughe replied,

A water-dragon.

Hope did not understand, because she had never heard of a dragon who lived in water, but she said that, nevertheless, they had to help Iggi.

Besides the fact that Iggi is getting water-logged and being bucked around, he does not seem to be in any immediate danger, replied Hughe. He went on,

If the water-dragon was a threat then why did the boat stop here? Surely its magic would not allow that, and besides, because of its size, the water-dragon could have caused us great harm.

"Then why did it attack Iggi?" Asked Hope.

Hmm, that is a good question, he said. *Did you not say that a similar situation happened when you first met Cal?* He asked. *That you thought he had purposely attacked you, when in truth he had simply misfired his arrow. Things are seldom what they seem,* he concluded.

Hope was embarrassed; it seemed so long ago.

"Then you are saying that it could be a misunderstanding?" Asked Hope.

Possibly, said Hughe, *but we will not know for certain until we rescue Iggi. I am just uncertain what the best course of action is to correct any misunderstanding*, he said.

It was true, thought Hope, Iggi did not seem any worse for the wear, except that he was drenched and would spend a lot of time drying off his wings. Maybe Hughe was right; maybe the water-dragon was surprised by the sudden intrusion and only wanted him off. Then why was it following them? These were questions that needed to be answered, but they would first have to calm down the water-dragon and get Iggi safely back on the boat.

"Hughe, if it is a water-dragon, does that mean you can communicate with it?" Asked Hope.

I do not know, he replied. *Although we come from the same species of reptiles, we are quite different. I can no more breathe underwater than the water-dragon can walk on land. Like humans, they may share a form similar to us, but they are quite different in looks and talents*, he said.

"We have to try," pleaded Hope.

I shall do my best, Hughe said, *but I am uncertain if it will work. The water-dragon is too distracted by its passenger for me to be able to contact it directly…maybe if we surprised it…*

Hope did not understand what Hughe meant as she watched Iggi being dunked over and over again in the water-dragon's desire to remove him from its back.

"Whatever you are going to do, do it now," said Hope, as she saw the water-dragon shaking Iggi back and forth while the fairy hung on tight. As Iggi reached out for Hope, who in turn tried to grab the fairy, Hughe sat concentrating silently, as the sun shining off his scales created a glow that surrounded him. Slowly the sun's rays reflected off the dragon's multi-colored scales as Hughe continued to concentrate. Brighter and brighter he became and his scales started to glimmer in iridescent colors until he began to fade into the background.

"You did it!" Exclaimed Hope, as she took her eyes off Iggi for a moment to witness this miraculous feat. Hughe was glad that his new-found talent had indeed worked, but for how long and for what purpose?

What good was it if he could not be seen? He thought.

Hope made contact with Hughe, feeling the dragon's perplexity about what to do next; she suggested that maybe if she could distract the water-dragon for a moment, she would be able to dislodge Iggi and get him on the boat. Hughe agreed, but still did not know how he could help. Hope started waving frantically at the creature. The water-dragon ignored her at first, choosing to concentrate on its passenger instead, but as Hope started to yell, its concentration was broken and it re-oriented on Hope. As it moved closer to the muse, Hope continued to wave frantically, hoping that by some miracle she would be able to grab Iggi. Closer and closer it came and, certain that the strange dragon was going to grab her, Hope made a last attempt to reach Iggi. Surprisingly, it worked, and she grabbed Iggi, who nearly fell into the water.

"It's about time!" He yelled, as he coughed up water. "Did it look like I was having a good time?" He stammered.

Hope ignored his outburst as the water-dragon approached them swiftly, having decided to continue its course toward them.

"Hughe," Hope yelled. Not knowing where Hughe actually was, she told the dragon that if he was going to do something, he better do it quick. The water-dragon was extremely close and, sensing the danger, Hughe pounced on it unexpectedly in order to make contact. The water-dragon was now even more confused as it looked around and saw no one on it but surely felt the extra weight. It raised its elongated body into the air and Hope now was certain of its size as it continued to stretch out completely. Hughe, feeling the strain of his unpredictable talent, and the panic that exuded from the water-dragon, concentrated on one word that he hoped it would understand: *"Friend."* The water-dragon blinked, as if surprised by this word coming out of nowhere, and stared blankly at the boat's passengers. Having calmed down enough for

Hughe to make contact, Hughe began to reappear, much to the surprise of the water-dragon. Shaking its head in disbelief, Hughe, who was still clinging on, explained that he was a dragon and that he and his friends meant it no harm, but had simply misunderstood its intentions. He quickly explained about their quest and this seemed to calm the water-dragon even more. The water-dragon told Hughe,

"My name is Splash, and I have been following you ever since you left the island."

Why? Asked Hughe.

"Forgive me," she said, "But I have never seen a multi-colored dragon before and I was curious about you. I did not know if you were as ferocious as I have heard, so I thought it was best to follow you without you knowing."

Being a dragon, Hughe understood; once again, their reputation had preceded them.

"I was about to approach you, when suddenly the strange elf grabbed onto my neck and I assumed I was being attacked. I am sorry for the misunderstanding," she said, blinking her eyes. "Can all land-dragons become invisible?" She asked.

Hughe shook his head. *No, as far as I know, I am the only one and I was only able to do it because of my strange coloring,* he said. *I cannot turn invisible,* he said, *it only appears that I do.*

Splash shook her head, not quite understanding and Hughe explained that his unique color enabled him to blend in with the background.

"You are quite a handsome specimen," she said, "Even more so with your unique coloring," and she seemed to coo.

Enough about me, Hughe said, wanting to change the direction of the conversation. *You still have not explained why you were following us?*

"Forgive me, where are my manners. As you know, my name is Splash, and yes indeed, I am a water-dragon. Long before humans started to walk the earth, dragons ruled the land."

Yes, Hughe said, *I know all of this but that does not explain why you were following us,* he persisted.

"Patience, mighty land-dragon, patience, and I will explain. Did you know that there was a dragon war?" She asked. Hughe had never heard of a dragon war and told her so. Splash assured him that there was and was not surprised that the land-dragons had not made this known to the younger hatchlings.

Go on, said Hughe, greatly interested.

"Dragons are territorial, as you know, and although the land was immense, it still was not enough for some." Hughe nodded, remembering how some of the other dragons felt and how his parentals' as leaders in the hierarchy had to deal with such disturbances.

"There was a group of dragons that did not agree with the territorial divisions and wanted more, so they would meet in secret to decide what to do," Splash said. "This caused great diversity among the dragons, an 'us versus them,' perception that led to great strife within the kingdom. It was decided that this could go on no longer and challenge was issued, which was agreed upon by both sides. A secret competition was held that would pit dragon against dragon, in the hope to gain more territory over which to rule. The competition was fierce, as each dragon challenged the opposite side in fire-breathing, rampaging, telepathic control and strength. As the competition continued, both side gained an advantage over the other for a long while, and the score continued to be even. Finally, there was no other choice but to pick an event that would determine the winner once and for all. After much discussion and disagreement, they decided that the fairest challenge to all would be one of endurance. All dragons have the ability to fly and so it was fair for both sides and neither could argue that they were at a disadvantage. However, only the strongest dragon who had practiced his flying skills well was able to accomplish this test of endurance. The rules were simple. Each chosen dragon would fly high above and hover for as long as he could, without using his other talents. As you are aware, it takes great concentration to fly and maintain a fixed position and poses a great risk to the dragon."

Hughe knew this was true, for it took all his strength just to fly from one position to another.

"The chosen dragons took their positions high above the clouds and, after a few moments to gather their thoughts, started the competition. As each one hovered above the ground, facing his competitor, each showed the strain it placed on their wings. Hour after hour, each side urged on its competitors as the challengers refused to withdraw, for they knew how important this competition was to them. Hours went by and as each competitor lost ground momentarily, it would be matched by the other and so it continued this way. Finally, after what seemed like days, but was actually only a matter of hours, one of the dragons touched ground and the competition ended."

Hughe understood that it was his side that had won and Splash agreed that was true.

I still do not understand how your people gained the ability to swim? He said. The water-dragon smiled and said that she would explain.

"After the competition, the losing side's competitor was crippled temporarily and it was decided that though they had lost the competition, nevertheless they were still part of the dragon kingdom, and should still retain some dignity. Thus, they were given the sea to rule in exchange for their loss of the land. After many centuries, we lost the ability to walk on land and fly and are only reminded of our former abilities and that secret competition by the wings you see on me."

Where are the others? Asked Hughe.

"I am not certain," replied Splash. "Like land-dragons, we are also territorial. Some have chosen to swim to deeper waters, seeking solitude, while others have chosen to search for abandoned mer-folk grottos in which to nest in hopes of attracting a mate."

Are you seeking a mate? Asked Hughe shyly.

The water-dragon seemed to blush at the land-dragon's question, which caused her normally black scales to become a pale pink.

"I am not certain exactly what it is I am looking for," replied Splash. "It is true that I am close to the age when females of my kind are searching for a mate, but I feel that there is so much more that I am searching for than to settle down and raise hatchlings."

Hughe understood. He too was destined to take a mate, but felt he had to discover himself first before taking on that responsibility. He suggested,

You are searching for your destiny.

"Yes, I am certain that is it," she replied. "Ever since I can remember, I could not help but think there was more to being a water-dragon then just raising hatchlings. I wondered what it is exactly that I am missing by not being a land-dragon," she said. "Do not misunderstand me, the sea is a wonderful and mysterious place, but is also very lonely," she said sadly. "I have always envied the land-dragons, who are masters of both land and air and have always hoped, if not for myself, but for my hatchlings, to give them that ability. I suppose I have been searching secretly for a way to do that, but it is rare for land-dragons to come near the ocean and those who do are simply passing high above and take no notice of me. No, I am almost certain that no land-dragon would willingly choose to be a companion of a water-dragon, giving up the land and air," Splash replied with a sigh.

Hughe now understood what he had suspected all along, what the older dragons were not willing to disclose. The reason the dragon kingdom was so secretive and unified whenever they heard dissention among the ranks was the simple fact that they knew what it had cost them so long ago. His parentals' would see to it that they did all that was in their power to avoid further division in order to prevent their destruction. That is why they stood united when Gap made his challenge to them for territorial rights, knowing he held the leverage he needed. He knew they would do anything to prevent the war that could end the dragons' lives as they knew it. Casualties of war were to be expected when such challenges were made, but not in daily life. No, this was far more dangerous, for it created division among the ranks and no one knew for sure what devastation it could bring if there was further division. Hughe had a thought. Maybe discovering why he was different was only part of his problem and something else was still needed to fulfill his true destiny: the re-unification of both species of dragons. No matter how much Gap complained about territorial rights, he would always be out-voted due to the loyalty of the water-dragons for welcoming them home, and of the others who felt betrayed by Gap's willingness to place his needs above the survival of the kingdom. Hughe noticed Splash looking at him, as she had no doubt that he was looking at her too and simply told her,

I would!

If not for the sea tears streaming from the water-dragon's eyes, they would have almost glazed over.

"You would do that for me?" She asked.

You are partially right; I would do it for us and our kingdom, Hughe replied. As he turned to face his companions who were looking at him, he realized his greatest challenge was still before him: saying good-bye.

Chapter 16:

SSSO LONG

"No, I don't understand," said Iggi, whose arms were folded across his chest while his tiny wings buzzed furiously. "First, nag-boy dumps us for ghost-girl and now basilisk-breath leaves us for the first sea-snake he sees who shows him her tail. Slitherina can use her snake charms on the wallet-with-fangs but it won't work on me! Who knows what's growing on her? I don't want any slimy scales growing on me," he said as he wiped his hands on the clothes he was wearing.

Iggi was so upset with what Hughe had told them that he turned away from his friend, who was desperately trying to make contact with him. Iggi turned one last time to face Hughe and Splash and told them,

"Leave me alone. I don't want what you have in case it's catching," and then he turned his back on his friend.

Hughe sat in the boat and Splash floated, bewildered, as Hope looked pleadingly at Iggi for understanding and compassion, but Iggi just sat staring silently at the open sea. Hughe was hurt by the fairy's words and as Hope touched him for a brief moment, she felt the pain the dragon was feeling.

"Hughe, are you alright?" She asked. Hughe was silent for what seemed like the longest time and Hope thought their contact was too brief and proceeded to touch him again.

I am fine, he said, *and although your first touch was brief, it was sufficient. Forgive me, dear friend, but I was momentarily distracted by my thoughts.*

"May I ask about what?" Hope asked. "If you mean because of the way Iggi was behaving, you know how he is and that he should be fine in a while."

Hughe looked at Hope and replied,

Maybe or maybe not.

"I do not understand." said Hope, perplexed.

Then I will try to explain, he said. *When we first started this adventure, I was lonely and confused because I was different from the others of my kind. I was frightened by those differences and had no one to turn to who would understand what I was going through. I only felt some assurance when you arrived on my island and rescued me from my loneliness. Only then did I realize that there were others facing similar despair and anguish. During this time we have become friends far beyond my expectations of what was possible from human-like species, all because we shared a common goal. We were all searching for understanding in a world where we believed there was none. I have been selfish,* he said.

"You have?" Asked Hope, surprised at the dragon's choice of words.

Yes, he said. *During our adventure to fulfill our destiny, we crossed a line somehow and became a family. That is how I think of all of you and hope you think that of me as well.*

"Of course we do," said Hope. Hughe was pleased by the muse's words and told her,

Then you will understand then that, in the true sense of the word, I have disappointed you. It is not enough to simply say the words, as it is the importance of our actions. Friends do whatever possible to ensure that the others' dreams are fulfilled and sacrifice their own dreams, expecting nothing in return.

Hope was beginning to understand what Hughe was implying, although she did not agree with him, and so she sat listening patiently to her friend.

I have fallen short of that by making my own dreams more important than yours, and I will not allow that to continue, even if it risks my own happiness. Iggi was hurt by Cal's sudden departure and was left alone and afraid without understanding why. I have learned that his words of anger are just that, mere words, and it is his actions that reveal his true self, Hughe said. *Iggi is hurt by my apparent abandonment of him in his plight, and for that I truly apologize. I will not abandon Iggi, as I know he will not abandon me. His feelings right now are more important than my own and I hope one day I am able to help myself, but for now that will have to wait.*

Hope was overwhelmed by the sadness of Hughe's words and the meaning behind them. As tears welled up in her eyes, she knew his words rang true, for how many times had she placed her feelings and desires aside for others. Her own sisters realized that Hope would do the same thing. They understood that they had to make the hard decision for Hope to leave, because she would not make it for herself. Hope found the courage in herself to ask Hughe if Splash agreed with his decision. Hughe looked at Splash, who gave a nod and slunk down deep into the water, her eyes barely visible. Hughe replied,

She is a dragon, though of a different variety, and will understand. Loyalty to others is prized above all else, no matter the difficulty it brings.

Hope looked at the water dragon's half-hidden eyes and saw her sadness at once again being alone. Hope asked Hughe if he was certain this was the best thing to do and if this was what he truly wanted?

No, replied Hughe, shaking his head, *but it is what is necessary.*

Hughe asked Hope.

Please let Iggi know I have had second thoughts about my decision, as I am sure the fairy will be obstinate about me making contact.

Iggi, who was still sulking in the corner of the boat as Hope approached him, demanded rudely,

"What do you want?"

Hope explained that Hughe had changed his decision to leave with the water-dragon and that he was sorry for any misunderstanding between them. He meant no disrespect toward Iggi and did not wish to abandon him and his problem. He had only been caught up in the moment when he first met Splash and had momentarily forgotten about the others. He had never seen a water-dragon before and in his excitement, forgot the reason he was here as well as the others. If Iggi would forgive him, Hughe would like to see to it personally that he and Hope fulfilled their destinies. Iggi was silent, which made Hughe and Hope think the fairy would not be so forgiving and only when he spoke abruptly did they realize there was a chance.

"Really? You think I'm a friend?" He asked.

"Yes, we do!" Replied Hope, knowing Hughe would agree. Iggi started to rub his eyes as if trying to get something out of them. Hope pretended not to see the stream of tears flowing down his cheeks.

"Must be something in the air," he mumbled as Hope and Hughe both noticed his blood-shot eyes. "You'd be willing to stay with me instead of helping scaly-bottom?" He asked.

Hughe looked at Splash with a pained expression on his face. For her part, she closed her eyes for a moment. Hughe replied,

Yes, that is what friends do for each other.

Iggi looked at Splash and then back at Hughe and said,

"Are you crazy, snooty? That water must've clogged your pea-brain as well as your ears."

Hughe, Hope and Splash all looked surprised at Iggi's remark, uncertain if they had heard him correctly. Iggi looked at Hughe directly and asked him,

"What makes you think I want to look at your ugly snout any longer than I have to?" He said. "It's bad enough I have to breathe your stale breath, let alone rub up against your scaly-hide. I have burns in places you wouldn't believe. Besides, I'm tired of picking up your shedding scales. It's disgusting," he smirked. "If the sea-snake can stand you, I say 'Good riddance,'" and he fell down rolling with laughter.

Hughe and Hope gaped at him, astonished by the fairy's words, and even Splash, whose body had remained hidden, rose in the air once again, stretching high. She could not believe what the stranger had done, and in her excitement, began to lick Iggi's face.

"Stop that!" He yelled, wiping his face, "Or I'll make a belt out of you!"

The water-dragon continued to lick his face, ignoring his protests, joyful at what the fairy had done for her.

"Ah, you're not so bad, I mean, if you like forked-tongues and all."

Hughe approached Iggi to show his appreciation, but Iggi side-stepped away from him.

"Don't get any ideas, snaggletooth," he said.

Hope giggled, as did Iggi. She could not help thinking that the little fairy was full of surprises. Hope gave Iggi a hug, which caught him off guard and he asked what it was for. Hope replied that she just felt like hugging him.

"Whatever," he said and then added quickly, "Thanks. So how's gila monster-boy and eel-girl going to leave? She can't fly and he can't swim."

Hope had also wondered about that. Hughe brushed up against her and said he thought he might have an answer.

Iggi is correct. There does seem to be an obstacle. However, I do believe I may have an answer. Although land-dragons technically are adept only on land and in the sky, I believe it may be possible for me to learn how to swim with Splash's help. In the event that I am unable to continue, I believe because of her size, she could easily carry me if the need arises. In return, I can carry her on land, I hope, and in time, if I become sufficiently strong, in the sky, and satisfy her curiosity about what she feels she is missing. As I learned from our quest quite early on, the assistance of others may be required to fulfil our destinies.

"Where will you go?" Asked Hope.

I must admit, Hughe replied, *that just as Splash is curious about the land and sky, I find myself strangely drawn to the mysteries of the sea. I am also curious to learn more about Splash's kingdom and hopefully find a solution that could once again reunite both our kingdoms. In time, I hope to return to my island with Splash and show that diversity is a strength, not a weakness, and that when we are divided, we really do risk the very foundations of our existence. I believe with Splash's assistance, as well as that of my parentals', we can accomplish this goal.*

Hope understood, as did Iggi, and both gave their approval to the dragon's decision. Hughe rubbed against Iggi for the last time and told him, This is not 'Good-bye' my friend, but 'Til we meet again,' and climbed on Splash's back, ready to depart.

"Whatever, puff," Iggi chuckled.

Hope and Iggi both waved to the dragons as they swam for deeper water. Farther and farther the dragons swam, while both Hope and Iggi continued to wave. Suddenly, both were startled by the voice they heard in their heads.

I am uncertain whether you can still hear me, but Splash has just informed me of a mer-girl she encountered a few days ago. She said she looked a little confused and disoriented and when Splash asked her what was wrong, the mer-girl replied that she was looking for something. She did not tell us sooner because she did not know we were looking for Sandy and Tuff. She is uncertain whether the mer-girl mentioned her name, but from her description she could indeed be Sandy. We will find out for certain if we are able to find her again, but at least that gives us some hope she survived. Good-bye, my friends, and good luck…

The thought became weaker and then it was gone. Iggi and Hope looked at each other in surprise, but this time it was Iggi who made the effort first as the two hugged in excitement.

Chapter 17:

THERE IS GNO ONE GNOME

ope still could not believe what they had just heard from
Hughe, that Splash had seen a young mer-girl who resembled
Sandy only days ago, and that the girl was looking for
something or someone. Could it have been Tuff the mer-girl was looking
for? Hope did not know for sure, because Splash herself only knew that
she had encountered a mer-girl who resembled their lost friend. Hughe
told them that, had Splash known, she would have made a greater effort
to speak to the mer-girl, but to her regret, she was occupied in following
what she was looking for, which coincidently happened to be Hughe.

The only thing Splash knew for certain was the way the mer-girl
was determined to find what she was looking for and kept diving and
reappearing in a different location. Hope believed from the description
the water-dragon gave Hughe that it was indeed Sandy, but why had
she not come looking for them? That was a question Hope wanted to
find out when they met again, but for now she could only wonder.
Hope was glad at the very least to know their friend had not drowned
in that terrible storm, as first suspected, and she shuddered at the
thought of her friend facing the blackness of the sea all alone. Hope
remembered the way she had panicked, gasping for breath as she
tried to retrieve Tuff, only to be carried away by the currents. She was

clinging desperately to whatever she could find, as wave after wave came crashing down around them and the swan boat sailed farther and farther away.

"Poor Sandy," she said as tears streamed down her face. Hope wiped away her tears as she looked at Iggi, who was busily eating until he noticed Hope staring at him in

bewilderment. Iggi swallowed what he had been eating quickly and said,

"I miss them too," and he lowered his eyes.

"We have to go back for them," pleaded Hope. Iggi wiped his mouth and choked out the words that Hope thought were left-over food in his mouth and replied,

"We can't!" Hope was shocked at the fairy's words and at first thought she had misheard him.

"You cannot mean what you are implying," she said, hoping she was correct in mishearing his words. "They are our friends," she said.

"Don't you think I know that?" Said Iggi. "Don't you think I want to find them too?" He said.

"I do not understand," she said. "Splash told Hughe that she saw Sandy and that she was desperately looking for someone or something and that has to be your best friend, Tuff." Iggi shook his head as his wings buzzed gently and found the words hard to say,

"No, she didn't."

"What?" Asked Hope, still not understanding.

"Splash only told Hughe that she had seen a mer-girl who looked like Sandy and that she was searching for something. Splash hadn't ever met us before and isn't sure it was Sandy, only that the description was similar to hers. For all we know, it's another mer-girl like Sandy who is on a quest. Splash only told Hughe that the mer-girl seemed lost and confused and wanted to find what she was looking for." He said, "If it's tuna-breath, then that means she's okay and Hughe and Splash will be looking for her.

Hope was not certain of the fairy's logic and asked how could he could be so sure.

"I can't," he said, "And neither can you, only that there's a chance and that we have to believe they're alright. I'm not the brightest fairy, but I believe we have to go on because if we don't, we may jeopardize everything we've done so far."

Hope looked at Iggi, whose eyes were turning red, and she knew his decision did not come easily. Hope turned to the swan boat, waiting for it to tell them that their decision was correct, but the swan boat was unusually silent and continued to sail. Hope agreed reluctantly.

"So what do we do now?" She asked.

Iggi said, "First, you'll eat and rest and hope that when our quest is over, all our questions will be answered."

The swan boat sailed on tirelessly as Hope and Iggi ate and slept, surrounded by the endless sea. Day turned into night and back again as it had so many times before, while its two passengers sat silent. Iggi stared off at the ocean while Hope read Clio's tome, hoping that somehow it would reveal what had happened to their friends. The tome gave no indication and only showed her in great detail what had transpired since she left her island. Startled by the boat's sudden honking, Hope looked up to see why it was making such a fuss.

"What's wrong with goose-feathers?" Asked Iggi, sounding like his usual self. Hope got up, looked where the swan boat was heading, and saw an island fast approaching.

"Look, an island," she said as she pointed in the direction they were heading.

"Don't tell me," Iggi muttered. "Here we go again." The boat kept honking as it made its way to the shore. Iggi, who was covering his ears because of the noise, grumbled that if the boat did not stop making so much fuss he was going to pluck its feathers one by one. Hope finally was able to calm the boat as it made its way to shore.

"That's better!" He said as he jumped off the boat to firm ground. "Where's here?" Asked Iggi, grappling with his sea legs.

"I don't know," said Hope, "But I am certain this is where we need to be. I think it might be best if we do some exploring."

"Uh uh, no way, sister! Don't tell me you've already forgotten what happens every time we go exploring?" He reminded her. "Someone ends up shooting arrows at us, or wants to eat us, or most important, I keep getting clobbered. If you want to explore, be my guest. As for me, I'm making camp right here," and Iggi sat down and refused to budge.

"What about the quest?" Asked Hope.

"I don't care about the quest!" He said stubbornly. "Flying or no flying, this fairy is staying grounded," and he crossed his arms.

Hope tried to persuade Iggi to change his mind, but the fairy refused. Even when his wings fluttered and buzzed, enjoying every opportunity to annoy him, he ignored them. Having no effect on him, Hope wasted no more time and decided to explore on her own. The path leading away from the shore was treacherous, as bramble bushes blocked her at every turn as she struggled to make her way through them. Slowly at first, Hope pushed her way past the bushes obstructing her view of what was hidden on the other side, and with great care so as not to get cut by the thorns, was beginning to make some progress. As the muse continued, the bushes that she had pushed away moments ago, snapped back into place, blocking her retreat. There's no turning back, thought Hope, and decided it was best to continue forward, as she could not go back the way she came. Her progress was slow and each step took her deeper into the obstructing tangle. Maybe this was a mistake, she thought. Maybe Iggi was right; all this could be for nothing. No. If that was true, then why would the boat have brought them here? Sometimes the answers are not so easily seen, as Hughe had said, but inside she wished Iggi had come with her. Hope pushed on even though she did not know why. Slowly, but surely, the bushes gave way until she was able to see a clearing. With one last push she got through and was startled by what she saw. Hope thought maybe she was just imagining it; maybe some dust had got in her eyes, but as she rubbed them, her vision did not change. Hope looked and saw a lush garden. Hope was surprised by its beauty and equally amazed that something so incredible could grow unattended. As Hope un-snagged a branch that clung to her tunic, she marveled at all the beautiful flowers and vegetables growing seemingly wild. She could not help but think that because of Iggi's stubbornness, he had missed a wonderful opportunity. Hope made her way down the winding garden path and noticed something she had not seen at first. In the garden were statues of little people carrying all sorts of garden tools; picks, axes, shovels and even wheelbarrows, while others held baskets filled with fruits and vegetables. Hope also noticed that some were even the size of Iggi, but they were wearing brightly-colored clothes and pointy hats. Hope looked around as she stood where the winding path ended and saw strange little cottages shaped like various fruits and vegetables. How odd. She wondered why whoever lived here would have so many statues placed unevenly around the garden. Hope's curiosity got the best of her and she began to examine each of the statues, which were incredibly lifelike. Hope looked closely at the first one and was amazed at its features; such detail was unheard of even on her island. She was surprised that the eyes seemed to follow her wherever she went. Hope continued to examine each of the statues in turn and noticed that they were of various ages. The older males had long, white beards that came to a point; the females were squat and wore long aprons that seemed to flow into a dress, while the younger ones, who were similarly dressed, resembled the older ones, and carried various garden tools and baskets of fruits and vegetables. How beautiful, Hope remarked once again.

"Certainly they have been tended as well as the garden," she said, admiring the craftsmanship. As Hope wandered through the garden admiring each statue in turn, she was startled by a yell as she looked up, she could see Iggi scrambling through the briars as she had done moments ago.

"Ouch, ouch, owww!" yelled Iggi, who seemed to be having even more trouble than Hope had. Finally, he arrived next to his friend Hope.

"This better be worth it," he said as he rubbed his bottom where the branches had stuck him.

"I thought you wanted to stay at camp," said Hope, trying to hide her joy at seeing him.

"Don't think I was scared or worried about you," he said. "I just didn't want you to get in any trouble, oh muse-less, and besides, who else is there to bail you out if you do," he grumbled. "Anyway, chicken-delight was squawking up a storm and I just couldn't take it anymore," he said, grinning.

Hope had learned early on in their adventure about taking Iggi at his word, and knew he did not mean half of what he said aloud. She was certain that he was concerned for her safety, which she greatly appreciated.

"What's up with all these statues?" Asked Iggi, who had just barely noticed them. "Don't tell me you've bored them stiff," he smirked. Hope ignored Iggi's comment as she had many times before, and told him there had to be a reason they were all out here. Iggi marched up to the closest statue and knocked it on its head with his fist.

"See, hard as a rock."

Hope warned him not to do that in case he broke one.

"I can't break it," said Iggi. "It's as hard as stone," and pummeled the statue once again with his fist to show her.

There is no use arguing with Iggi, thought Hope. Once he was in that mood there was no stopping him.

"Come on," said Hope. "We have to figure out why the swan boat brought us here. Hope turned around and was about to make her way to the cottage she had seen when she first arrived, while Iggi could still be heard saying,

"It's just stone." Hope continued toward the cottage when, out of nowhere, she heard Iggi yell,

"Ouch!" Hope turned around and was surprised to see Iggi sitting on the ground rubbing his head.

"What is wrong now?" She asked.

"That stupid statue hit me," he said, still rubbing his head. Hope looked at the fairy in disbelief, and told him that was impossible.

"Statues do not hit people on the head. You must be imagining it."

"Well, then my imagination has a great left hook," he said and Iggi continued to stare at the statue, which was in the same position as it had been moments before, but Iggi could swear this time it was grinning at him. Iggi brushed himself off and pushed the statue hard with both hands. Hope thought for sure it would topple over, but amazingly, it returned to its previous position. She headed back towards the cottages. Iggi turned to look at her and in the next moment fell to the ground and yelled,

"Hey!" Hope turned when she heard the fairy yelling and once again saw Iggi on the ground. This time, though, she was startled to see the statue looming over him. This time there was no doubt in her mind that Iggi was correct that the statue was alive, for right before her very eyes it had changed positions, crossing its hands and smiling.

"I told you that statue's alive," he said as he got up and dusted himself off once again, being very careful this time to keep his distance from the statue.

Hope looked in amazement at the statue, which stood immobile, and told Iggi again,

"But that is impossible."

"Impossible?" Grumbled Iggi. "I don't think so. Being conked on the head once might've been an accident, but being pushed was another thing altogether," he said. Iggi stared eye to eye at the statue, examining it very closely and made faces at it, trying to see if it blinked. Hope could not believe what she was witnessing, as Iggi did everything he could think of to see if the statue would move; he even made faces at it.

"Don't play games," he shouted at the statue. "I know you're alive," he said adamantly, and stomped his feet. Hope could not help giggling at the sight of Iggi poking and prodding the statue in the hope of making it move. It was getting late and Hope wanted to find out who lived here and why they had all these statues. Finally, she told Iggi this was getting them nowhere.

"Yeah, you're right," he said, still eyeing the statue carefully. "This is probably nothing more than a perch for harpies," he said and as he turned to follow Hope, shoved the statue once more. Iggi had his back to the statue when Hope looked around and saw the statue push Iggi to the ground as before.

"What the heck!" He yelled. "*Now* tell me you didn't see that."

Hope assured him she now believed him, as the statue, which had its arms folded moments before, now seemed to be pointing and laughing at Iggi. Hope realized the mistake they had made; they were looking for the person or persons who lived here, never realizing they had been here all along as living statues. If that was true and she had no doubt it was, then why did the others not move as this one most certainly did?

"Iggi, could you please come here?" She asked, as Iggi continued to make faces at the statue.

"What?" He asked as his tiny wings started to buzz, indicating that he was getting annoyed.

"Iggi, I think it is best if you come here right now," she said, but Iggi ignored her as he fumbled in his knapsack and retrieved a strange tool.

"What is that?" Asked Hope.

"It's a chisel," said Iggi, grinning. "I'm going to find out what this statue is made of."

A look of horror crossed Hope's face because she was certain he meant it. As Iggi continued grinning, he told her, or was it the statue, that a big piece was what was needed. As Iggi started to come closer, the statue panicked, came fully to life and started to yell.

"No cousin!" Shouted the statue, which was now very much alive. "You do not mean it," and started to run away.

"Ah ha," said Iggi triumphantly. "So you're alive, are you? Well, just for hitting me on the head, I'm going to chisel that grin right off your face," and Iggi started to chase the funny little man around the garden.

Hope was surprised by the statue's sudden mobility, and if not for the seriousness of Iggi's threat, it would almost have been comical.

"Help me!" Pleaded the funny little man to Hope. "My cousin means to cause me great harm." Then he tripped and fell on the ground.

"Now I got you," said Iggi. "And quit your fussing. I just want to see what you're made of and don't call me cousin!" Iggi raised the chisel and Hope, seeing the determination in Iggi's eyes, rushed to the little man, which infuriated Iggi.

"Who are you," she asked, "And why did you attack Iggi?" The little man's eyes were filled with panic as he eyed the chisel that Iggi still held in his hand. Hope looked at Iggi and asked him to put it away. The fairy grumbled that she never let him have any fun.

"Whatever," said Iggi, as he placed the tool back in his knapsack, "But if he gives us anymore trouble I'm going to start whittling." The little man smiled gratefully as he jumped up and started to dust himself off.

"Thank you, oh thank you, kind lady," while he kept an eye on Iggi and rushed to stand next to Hope.

"I gknew from the moment I saw you with my cousin that you were a kind and gentle soul," he said.

"Harpy dung," yelled Iggi, fumbling in his knapsack. "And stop calling me cousin, or I'm going to start carving my initials into your thick skull. Answer her or else," said Iggi irritably.

"Oh yes, oh yes, cousin. Anything you say. I gknew from the moment I saw you that you were a man of your word."

"Whatever," said Iggi. "Now tell us who you are and what's up with all these statues?" He demanded. The funny little man saw the way Iggi was clutching his knapsack and knew that he was serious and that when all else failed, he needed to tell the truth.

"My name is Gnorm and I am a garden gnome, and these 'Statues' as you call them , are garden gnomes as well, but as you can plainly see, I am the only one able to move. My responsibility is to harvest the honey from the bee hives."

"What happened to the others?" Asked Hope.

"Yeah," said Iggi suspiciously, "Why can't the others move?" He asked.

"I am uncertain," Gnorm replied sadly. "Gnormally we do our work at gnight and only become animated at dusk, and then during the day we are as you see us, living statues. But for some strange reason, I am the only one who can become animate at will."

"Couldn't they be resting during the day?" Asked Iggi, and Hope nodded in agreement because she was wondering the same thing. The gnome shook his head sadly and explained he had thought the same thing at first, but when gnight came they remained the same.

"That is why, cousin…" Iggi looked at Gnorm and grumbled, and the gnome said quickly, "Kind sir, I was surprised to see you moving about and gknocked on your head to see if you were a gnome, but on closer inspection I realized you were only kin," he said sadly.

"Are you saying that you alone have been taking care of the garden?" Hope asked. Gnorm nodded and said it was a struggle, but she was correct.

"How sad," replied Hope, and asked when he first noticed this was happening.

"It started about one month ago, about the time these strange instruments started washing up on shore. At first gno one paid them any attention, because we are garden gnomes and have gno use for musical instruments, but soon our curiosity got the best of us, and as they did gnot seem dangerous, we kept them. The children were the first to go, as they made their way to the beach in the hope of finding the instruments, while the adults remained behind tending to their duties. When the children did gnot come home as expected, we sent out a search party and discovered that something terrible had happened to them."

"Oh, nó, how awful!" Cried Hope.

"One by one, our children were being turned to stone, and as each gnew discovery was made, we brought them to the garden for safe-keeping. Eventually, the adults also became affected by this strange occurrence, until just I and my gnu were left."

Iggi looked puzzled, because he had only thought that the three of them were there.

"A gnu?" Asked Iggi. "What's a gnu?"

"I do gnot gknow, what is a gnu with you?" Said the gnome, and started laughing hysterically. "You fell for that one, cousin. Sorry," said Gnorm, trying not to smile, "Laughter is the only thing that keeps me going." The gnome chuckled.

"Whatever!" Said Iggi irritably, as his tiny wings started to buzz in anger.

"Huh? What is that? Sounds like the bees are upset," said Gnorm. Hope assured the gnome that it was no such thing and pointed to Iggi's back. Gnorm looked where Hope had pointed and saw Iggi's two tiny wings buzzing angrily.

"Well, look at that," exclaimed the gnome. "Can I touch them?" He asked.

"No, you can't!" Iggi replied.

Gnorm had never seen wings before and, ignoring Iggi's warning, tried to touch them.

"Stop that!" Said Iggi.

"Well, cousin," Gnorm said. "I knew you were special, but I gnever realized how special. Those are some gnice wings."

Iggi grumbled as he moved out of Gnorm's reach and the wings started to buzz more softly at the gnome's compliment. Iggi's annoyance was becoming more apparent and he tried to change the subject.

"So how can we help you, if you can't help yourself?" Asked Iggi. "We have our own problems."

Gnorm, who was still staring at Iggi's wings, was startled by his comment.

"You do?" Asked the gnome.

"Yes, we do," Iggi said.

"If I may ask, what kind of problems could you both have?" Asked Gnorm.

Hope quickly made introductions and explained that they were on a quest to fulfill their destinies.

"Well, well, well," said Gnorm. "I gnew, but I gnever thought you could be on a quest."

"Uh uh," said Iggi shaking his head. "Cut the malarkey already," he said as he pointed his finger at the gnome. "You'd think you were a leprechaun or something."

"Ah," said Gnorm, whose eyes lit up hearing the word "Leprechaun." "So, you gnow of our cousins, do you?" He grinned. "I gnew from the moment I saw you, cousin, that you were a wise man."

Iggi shot the gnome a look and asked him, "Why do you keep calling me cousin? I'm not your cousin, and of course I know of leprechauns."

The gnome became quite serious and replied that Iggi was quite mistaken and his wings proved it. Gnorm explained that a long time ago they had derived from the same folks but, because of a curse, had evolved into their own unique forms.

"Curse? What curse?" Asked Iggi. "I haven't heard of any curse."

"Ah, but there was one so long ago and you are gnot as alone as you might think."

This led Iggi to wonder. They did look similar, except for his wings and the funny clothes Gnorm was wearing.

"Whatever," said Iggi less enthusiastically than Hope had ever heard him say anything before. "Just don't expect any birthday cards," he huffed.

"Come, and I will explain," said the gnome, and Hope and Iggi followed Gnorm into one of the strange little houses they saw when they first arrived in the garden.

Chapter 18:

FAMILY AFFAIR

Gnorm invited Hope and Iggi for dinner and to stay the night and was busily preparing the food as they warmed themselves by the fireplace. Occasionally, they would hear Gnorm banging pots and pans in the kitchen. Hope offered to help him, but the gnome just chuckled, saying it was a pleasure to have some real guests for a change. Gnorm rushed out to set the table and placed the dishes for each course. Hope had noticed Iggi staring off into the fireplace and asked him if anything was wrong.

"Huh?" Replied Iggi nonchalantly. "Oh nothing, I was just thinking to myself."

Hope sensed sadness in Iggi's words as Gnorm loudly clanged dishes as he placed them on the table.

"Almost done," he said and rushed back into the kitchen before anyone could reply. Hope asked Iggi if what the gnome had said upset him in any way. Iggi looked away from the fire and stared into Hope's eyes and then looked back into the fireplace.

"No," Iggi said, "Not really. I just can't believe what he said. I think he's just crazy with loneliness," he said, continuing to stare into the fireplace.

"You mean about the two of you being cousins?" Asked Hope.

Iggi sadly replied, "Yeah."

"But I think it is great," said Hope.

"You really do?" Asked Iggi.

"Of course I do," replied Hope. "This is what you have always wanted, is it not, a place to belong."

"What about my quest, and finding out why I'm so big and can't fly?" He asked.

Hope could not help but smile at Iggi and explained that maybe he misunderstood his quest.

"What?" He said. "Don't tell me you've gone crazy too. All I've ever wanted to do was fly like the other fairies," he said as his tiny wings buzzed in agreement.

"I know that is what you wanted," she said, and placed her hand gently on Iggi's shoulder, "But as we have learned, what we want may not be what we truly need," she said.

"I don't understand," said Iggi as he leaned closer to Hope in order to not miss what she was saying.

"Maybe," she said, "What you are truly looking for is not just a place to belong, but a family in which to make a difference."

"A family?" Iggi shook his head in disbelief, uncertain if he had misheard what Hope was saying. Hope, seeing the confusion in his eyes, told him she would explain. Gnorm was still banging plates down on the table and said,

"Be ready in a minute," and dashed back into the kitchen.

Hope smiled as the gnome returned to the kitchen and turned her attention back to Iggi, who was still scratching his head.

"Are you telling me you do not see the resemblance between you and the gnomes?" Asked Hope.

Iggi was startled by the question and then replied, "Yeah, I guess so."

Hope nodded, knowing she had his attention, and said, "So you know it is possible you could be…" and before Hope could finish her words, Iggi replied,

"Cousins?"

"Yes, cousins," she said.

"In case you haven't been paying attention during this adventure, I'm a fairy, not a gnome," he said. "It's impossible."

"The world is full of possibilities. Anything is possible," said Hope.

"I don't get you," Iggi said.

"Then I will explain," said Hope, and she proceeded to tell Iggi, hoping to find a way he would understand. "Cal is a centaur-boy, but his ancestry comes from a cross-breed of human and horse. While his near-sightedness was improbable, it was not impossible," Hope said. "Sandy herself was a cross-breed between human and fish," she said, but Iggi was chuckling at the thought of humans and fish mating.

"Obviously it must've been due to falling in a love spring," he said.

Hope, sensing what Iggi was chuckling about simply said,

"Love has no boundaries."

Iggi grinned and said,

"Love springs eternal, huh," and laughed.

Hope was glad for once that she did not understand his sense of humor. Hope also pointed out the fact that although Hughe and Splash were obviously both dragons, each species evolved into their own.

"Family, huh?" Asked Iggi. "Isn't it bad enough I have to worry about the fairy-folk laughing at me behind my back. Now I also have to worry about the gnomes, pixies, elves and everyone else in existence," he huffed.

Hope knew he was only seeing the negative side of her argument and quickly explained he had missed the point. Hope said,

"Your problem all along was that you were surrounded by too much negativity and you believed it. A family is not so much the one that you are born into, as it is the love and respect of those around you. Yes, you are different from the other fairies, but that is what makes you special," she said.

Hope explained that on her island, all her sisters were different in looks and talent and that it is something to value, not to feel ashamed of.

"It is those differences that are our strength, not our weakness," she said.

Iggi was listening intently, as Hope well knew, and she had to make sure he understood the point she was making.

"Did you not tell us that you chose to live in a cave away from the other fairies that they did not ask you to leave?"

Iggi's face dropped at hearing Hope's words and he said,

"But they were making fun of me."

Now it was Hope's turn to laugh and she replied,

"But that is what families do. Did you think that meant they did not love you? Now you have the perfect chance to make a difference in someone's life. Maybe you truly did misunderstand your quest. As I said, what we want is not necessarily what we truly need."

Iggi sat in shock at what she was implying and could only mumble his reply,

"You mean, stay here?"

"Yes," said Hope, "If that is what you want to do." She was glad that Iggi understood at last.

Gnorm was finally through and announced that dinner was ready. Hope and Iggi seated themselves at the wooden table. Hope looked around and noticed a pot of tomato soup, a vegetable salad and stuffed artichokes. Gnorm apologized for not having a dessert for them but that he had been so busy tending the garden he forgot to pick some mushrooms. Iggi did not care, which was obvious by the way he was shoveling the food onto his plate.

"Mmmmm," he said.

"Mushrooms?" Asked Hope quizzically.

"Yes," said Gnorm, "Mushroom ice-cream is a gnome specialty."

"I've never heard of it," said Iggi. "Could you pass me some more soup?"

Hope gave Iggi a look, but the fairy knew better than to look back at her and continued slurping his soup.

"I sure wish I had some," said Gnorm.

Hope looked again at Iggi, who was eating an artichoke and he replied,

"Okay, be right back."

Iggi retrieved his knapsack, brought it back to the table and presented the fairy mushrooms to Gnorm.

"Will these do?" He asked.

Gnorm looked at the fairy mushrooms' brilliant colors and his face nearly turned white.

"Where did you find those?" Asked Gnorm nervously.

Iggi told him he had picked them a while ago, when he first met Hope, and these were all that were left. Gnorm quickly got up from his seat and inspected the colorful mushrooms closely.

"What is wrong?" Hope asked.

"They're not poisonous," said Iggi. "Here, see for yourself?" And he held out the fairy mushrooms to the gnome. The gnome jumped back so quickly, startled by Iggi's gesture, that he almost fell over.

"What's wrong with you?" Iggi asked. "It's not like I'm going to poison you," he said.

"Gnot purposely," said Gnorm, shaking, "But maybe by accident."

Hope and Iggi looked at each other and then at Gnorm, who noticed their looks of confusion and told them he would explain. Gnorm began,

"A long time ago, all of the magic folk looked the same and were the same size, but soon that all changed. It was a dark time, when good and evil coexisted might versus magic if you will."

"Oh great," said Iggi. "A drama queen." Hope gave Iggi a quelling look and the fairy quieted down.

"As I was saying," said Gnorm, "Good people ruled the kingdom because of their overwhelming numbers, but bad ones were scheming to change all that.

Hope and Iggi sat fascinated as Gnorm continued his tale.

"As I have told you, cousin, once we were all the same, but that does gnot mean that we were all on the side of good. Anyway, those seeking power decided that something needed to be done. After much discussion, they agreed that a spell was gneeded. There was a disagreement, however, on how it should be done," he said. 'Poison the water supply,' some said. But others were worried that it would poison them as well by eventually leaking into their supply. They finally decided what they needed to do, something subtle that would only affect the good people."

Iggi unconsciously reached for a handful of fairy mushrooms and, realizing what he was about to do, quickly snatched his hand back.

"The mushrooms?" Asked Iggi.

"Yes," Gnorm nodded, glad to see that his cousin understood. "But gnot just any mushrooms: *fairy* mushrooms. Those who sought control gknew that the way to their enemy's hearts was through their stomachs. Everyone was in agreement, and after gathering some ordinary mushrooms, they concentrated their curse upon them and, to prevent one of their own from eating them, they made them easily recognizable. Oh, they were clever indeed. How the mushrooms glistened and shined with their bright colors. They were certain they would attract any unwary eye. The next thing they did was to grind up the cursed mushrooms and scatter them in the wind in the direction of their enemies," he said. "Oh, how they celebrated that terrible gnight, gknowing they had succeeded in unbalancing the power in their favor."

A look of horror came over Hope's face and she replied,

"How terrible!"

Iggi shook his head in disbelief.

"But I thought that was just a fairy-tale to keep the children in line," he said.

"Have you gnot listened to a word I have said, cousin? Impossible or gnot, the deed was done," Gnorm said sternly. "Even fairy-tales have some truth to them," he added.

"What's this have to do with me?" Asked Iggi. "I'm perfectly fine," he grumbled.

Hope was wondering the same thing and then she realized her mistake. The gnome noticed her look and replied,

"I see you are starting to understand," he nodded approvingly. "The fairy mushrooms were only supposed to upset the balance of power, but even the evil ones gnever realized the added effect. The good people discovered too late what was happening, and realized the strange mushrooms were cursed. By having discovered these strange mushrooms and eaten them, they started to change, and it became obvious to those around them that the effect was permanent. Each one started taking on different forms and eventually evolved into what are gnow gknown as pixies, elves, gnomes, leprechauns and fairies."

That's why I'm four-feet tall?" Exclaimed Iggi.

"Yes," said Gnorm, "And I suspect that is what caused your dilemma."

Now Iggi wasn't the brightest, but he started to figure out why there was such an abundance of the fairy mushrooms and why no other fairies had eaten them.

"Yes," said Gnorm. "They gknew they were cursed."

"But why didn't they tell me?" Asked Iggi.

I suspect they did gnot gknow you had discovered them and, had they gknown, it would have been too late. The good people realized their mistake too late and though the change was permanent, they swore they would do gno other harm and cast them far away, hoping this would prevent others from eating them. Until you discovered them," he added sadly.

"Near your cave," said Hope, "They probably had forgotten they were there."

"So that's why I'm so big," said Iggi in amazement.

Gnorm eyed Iggi, as if realizing for the first time that Iggi was big for a fairy. Then he shook his head,

"Gno."

This infuriated Iggi so much that his tiny wings started to buzz furiously.

"Don't you shake your head at me, you gnarly old troll," he said. "You just said it was because I ate the fairy mushrooms."

Once again, Iggi was losing control, and Hope did her best to calm him, asking the gnome,

"Then what did you mean about the mushrooms not being the reason Iggi is so big?"

Still shaking his head, Gnorm tried to explain, while Iggi sat staring at the gnome.

"My cousin is so big because that is what he was meant to be," said Gnorm. "I told you we had all been the same in looks and size at one time and gnot even the curse accounted for that. So Iggi is big because of our ancestors."

"You mean because of genetics?" Asked Hope. She explained that her sisters Flora and Fauna had introduced this science to the human world and, although she did not understand it fully, she understood that it had to do with something called recessive genes. Iggi and Gnorm both scratched their heads and Hope said that, although science was not her favorite subject, she would try to explain it. Flora and Fauna had taught her that all living things derived from one, much like what Gnorm had said about him and Iggi being cousins.

"Occasionally," she said, "Because of a recessive gene, the offspring of plants and animals can be quite different than the parents."

Iggi said, "Huh?"

"Remember when I was telling you about Sandy and Cal having been the result of cross-breeding?" She reminded him.

"Yeah, but I don't see what that has to do with it," he said.

"Although their relatives cross-bred and produced an entirely new species, it is still possible that, due to a recessive gene, they could produce an offspring much like one of the originals," she said. "Take Cal, for instance. Centaurs acknowledge, though reluctantly in mixed company, that their ancestors were humans. Cal was the first centaur who ever forced them to realize that his defect was the result of a recessive gene that traced back to their ancestry."

Iggi began to understand and asked Hope,

"So, is my size due to a recessive 'Whatchamacallit'?"

"Yes," she said, "And it is quite possible that your offspring may be able to fly."

"But that still doesn't explain why I can't fly," he said.

Hope looked to Gnorm and asked,

"Could the mushrooms be affecting his wings?"

Gnorm nodded and said,

"Yes, the curse could have made them small."

"Are you telling me because I've been eating these fairy mushrooms all this time, that's the reason I can't fly?" He asked.

"Yes, cousin," Gnorm said. "I suspect you were always been meant to fly, but because of those cursed things, your wings could gnot grow to the size they were meant to be. I believe if you just stop eating them, that in time your wings will return to gnormal."

Iggi could not restrain his enthusiasm and jumped so high the other two could almost believe he was flying.

"You mean it?" He grinned as he landed back on the ground.

Hope was excited for her friend, but knew this meant the end of their adventure together.

"Hope, I can't believe it, I couldn't have done it without you!" Iggi said.

Hope looked at him and, as their eyes met, he realized this meant his journey was over.

"Hope, I didn't mean, I mean, uh…" he said.

Hope hugged her fairy friend and said she understood, but that just because his journey was at an end, it did not mean they would stop being friends.

"Until the day we can end this curse, Gnorm needs to be around family so that he would not feel that he has to go through this alone. Do you understand?" Asked Hope.

Iggi, not one for emotions, replied that he did and as Hope made her way to the bedroom for some much needed rest, she heard Iggi say, "And I'll miss you too Hope."

Chapter 19:

JOURNEY'S END

Morning came soon enough, with the first rays of dawn shining into the little house. It reminded Hope of home. How she had missed her sisters during this journey. She wondered if they had missed her, but of course knew the answer to that question already. Hope did not know how long she had been away from the island, because the problem for a muse was that time had a way of standing still. In her heart, though, she felt that even one more day was too long. Hope pondered all that had happened to her on her adventure: how she met Sandy, whose only wish was to be with her family and, due to the great storm that had caught them all off guard, was lost at sea along with Iggi's best friend, Tuff. She thought of how they had watched helplessly as Sandy sacrificed herself to retrieve the little rag doll, while the rest of them had scrambled to safety on Hughe's back. Hope felt terribly guilty about losing Sandy and, in the end, what had it accomplished? Both were lost to the sea forever.

Cal, on the other hand, had found a place to belong with the invisible giantess named Enigma, and Hughe found happiness with Splash. And now it appeared that Iggi, too, had discovered his home. Still, Hope felt terrible about losing Sandy and Tuff. How she had wished they all could have found what they were seeking, even if that meant she failed in her own quest.

Hope remembered what her sister Clio had told her about taking responsibility for her actions, but that only made her feel worse. Hope knew that she would have to find a way to tell Sandy's parent's of their daughter's fate; perhaps the swan boat could help her. Hope heard Gnorm in the kitchen clanging pots and pans as he made them breakfast, and occasionally she heard Iggi talking to his wings, telling them,

"Hurry up and grow already."

Hope went to the living room and, as she had thought, saw Gnorm and Iggi preparing breakfast.

"What took you so long?" Asked Iggi, still excited from the night before, "I thought orc-boy and I would have to douse you with water or something. Don't tell me you've been up all night again," he said.

Hope shook her head and said no, she was just thinking about the quest. She decided not to tell them about her guilt over Sandy and Tuff. Iggi, though, having spent so much time with her since their first meeting, knew what it was that was making her sad.

"Don't try to fool me," he said. "Not after all we've been through."

Hope had to admit that Iggi was correct. Friends did not lie to each other, even if it hurt; so she told Iggi and Gnorm about her guilt over losing Sandy and Tuff.

"I know," said Iggi. "I miss them too, but scaly-bottom said she saw a mer-girl who looked like Sandy and gecko-rear said they would look for them. You taught us not to give up, Hope, so I'm reminding you the same thing. We knew the risk and we chose to take it."

Hope was amazed by Iggi's thoughtful response and pleased to see that, at the very least, he had let down his guard. Gnorm asked Hope to stay with them, but Hope politely declined, telling them,

"I have to go home and let my sisters know I am no better off than I was before. I am still a talentless muse."

"Nope, you are better off" said Iggi. "You may be talentless, but you're not friendless."

This made Hope smile. After breakfast, she helped clear the table and then had to say her goodbyes. As much as Hope would have liked to stay, she had a responsibility to let her sisters know of her adventures and to find Sandy's parents. Hope hugged Gnorm and Iggi, then boarded the swan boat and reminded them that she would help them find a way to break the curse.

Hope asked the boat to take her where she was needed most and, with a honk, the golden swan boat sailed away. Days passed as Hope ate the food Gnorm had given her for her journey. She wished she could have helped him, but as yet, she had no idea how. Maybe her sisters, being older, knew how to lift the curse. Thinking about that made Hope feel better. During the night, while the swan boat sailed on, Hope dreamed of her quest and the friends she had made, and slept comfortably, knowing she had done her best. Had her sisters not told her that it is better to have tried and failed, then never to have tried at all? But what did this mean for her?

Here she was a muse, a goddess of inspiration yet she lacked the talent to inspire others. How could she live with this fact and what use could she be to her sisters? Hope became sad at this thought and wondered whether her sisters would even accept her back, knowing that she had not found her destiny? That night, Hope cried herself to sleep and wished she had found a way to keep this secret to herself, but it was no use; having a sister who could see the future made it difficult to keep secrets. Sooner or later, they would have found out, but Hope wished it could be later, much later. Hope slept deeply, and began to wake up only when she heard the boat honking incessantly.

"What is it?" She asked. But the boat kept honking, much as it did whenever they were close to where they needed to be, some unknown destination.

"Are we there?" She asked, but the boat kept honking to make sure she stayed awake. Hope wiped the sleep from her eyes and looked around. For a moment she was not sure what she was seeing. Straight ahead was an island that looked vaguely familiar and as the boat sailed closer, there was no denying it. Just ahead lay the island of Leisha. Hope was finally home, but that could not be true, the boat must have made a mistake. The boat, hearing her thoughts, honked in disagreement. This was where she was needed most. If Hope had doubts, they soon vanished when she saw that all of her sisters had come to welcome her home. Although she was no more than a hundred yards from shore, to Hope it seemed thousands of miles away, and she urged the boat to sail faster. Hope could barely restrain herself as the boat docked.

Clio was the first to greet her little sister and hugged her so tight Hope could scarcely breathe. She did not care, though, because she was home.

"Clio," said Flora and Fauna in unison, "Just because you are the oldest, it does not give you the right to be selfish with our little sister."

Hope could not help but laugh, as did the other muses, as each in turn welcomed their sister home.

"I do not understand." said Hope. "How did you know I would return today?"

But then Hope knew the answer; Delphi had foreseen it, of course.

"I am a little confused," said Hope. "Why did the boat bring me home? Did its magic fail?"

The muses smiled and Clio told her, as she rubbed the swan boat's neck, that the boat did not fail, but performed its service admirably. The swan boat seemed to puff up its chest at hearing the compliment and turned from gold to a reddish tint.

"I still do not understand," she said. "I thought its magic had to take me where I was needed most."

"You misunderstand, little sister," said Clio. "You are where you are needed most, with your family."

Hope could hardly believe it, but of course the boat brought her to where she was needed most, this time back to her loving family.

"I have so much to tell you," said Hope.

"All in good time, little sister, but for now, you need to rest."

Hope did as her sister told her, but was too excited to sleep and decided instead to explore the island which she had called home for centuries. Hope still thought she might be dreaming and found she had to touch everything, still uncertain of its reality. Hope finally came to the conclusion that it was not a dream and that she was home where she belonged. Time passed quickly and soon it was time to eat in the great hall. While she tried to eat, her sisters bombarded Hope with all sorts of questions.

"What was it like?" Asked Nia.

"Were you scared?" Signa asked.

"Was Iggi really a grouch?" Asked Flora and Fauna.

Hope told her sisters everything and the things she forgot would be written in great detail in the magic tome Clio had given her. Her sisters knew Hope was as glad to be home as they were to have her home. Still, they noticed that something seemed to be troubling her.

Clio asked, "Is something wrong, little sister?"

Hope told her about Sandy and Tuff, how they had been lost at sea during a terrible storm and how horrible it was to see her friend drown. Then she began to cry.

"Drown? Really?" Said a voice. "My, that is indeed horrible."

Hope could not believe one of her sisters would say such a thing, and as she looked up to see who it was, once again she could not believe her eyes.

"Sandy!" She cried. "But how? We saw you. I mean, I saw you drown."

Hope was confused and, seeing her friend's startled look, Sandy explained quickly.

"Remember how terrible that storm was and the way the boat kept rocking and I kept hugging Tuff so tightly? Well I have to tell you, Hope. That was the best thing that ever happened to me."

"It was? I do not understand," said Hope once again. "How could something like that be the best thing that has happened to you?"

"I have to be honest," said Sandy. "I was scared, but even more so when the wave snatched Tuff from me and carried him out to sea. I knew if I did not get him back, Iggi would never forgive me. So I had no choice but to go after him, and then I started to panic as the boat got farther away, and I thought I was going to drown."

"We all did," said Hope.

"The problem was that the sea-quake that took me away from my parents at birth frightened me so much I forgot that I could breathe in water. I was too young to remember that I was a mer-girl and at that moment I stopped panicking and went after Tuff, but I was too late. The closer I got to him, the farther away you were and by the time I realized that, you were gone. Thanks to you, Hope, I am no longer afraid of water, and it is also because of you that my family and I are together again."

"I am so happy," said Hope, as both girls hugged and started to cry.

"I am too," Sandy said.

"I am so glad everyone found what they were looking for, even if I did not fulfill my destiny," Hope said sadly.

Sandy reminded Hope that, had it not been for her, they would still be no better off, that without Hope's unselfishness towards others' needs, they would still be lonely and isolated from the world. It was then that her sisters pointed out a fact that Hope had forgotten. They reminded her of all the good she had done for them as well as others, helping those who could not help themselves by just being a friend. Hope learned from her sisters how truly special she was and that she did, indeed, possess an important talent. Bursting with excitement, Hope pleaded with her sisters to tell her what it was. They said that it was obvious to everyone but her that her special talent was in bringing lonely people together so that they were no longer lonely. They explained that this talent was unique and much needed in the world, by both gods and mortals.

"That is why," Delphi explained, "This is not the end, but the beginning of a new chapter in your life."

"I do not understand," said Hope.

"I have foreseen the future and there are others who need your special talent."

"When?" Asked Hope.

Knowing that her sisters and Sandy were anticipating the answer equally, Delphi replied, "Soon, very soon," and smiled.

ABOUT THE AUTHOR

Tyger B. Dacosta was born in San Jose, California and was given up for adoption at birth. Raised by adoptive parents in Santa Clara County, his new family never understood his need for writing. Like the heroes in his stories, Tyger believed in happy endings and imagined what his parents were like and if they ever thought of finding him. He did not realize that, while living in San Francisco, his dream was about to come true; with the help of his friend John, he was finally reunited with his family. Tyger enjoys working on children's issues and has spoken at the legislature on adoption. He hopes to adopt a child of his own one day, but until then continues to write books and is working on: *The Dragon Prince, Cats-Eye, The Caterpillar Princess, The Littlest Giant* and *The Blue Djinn*. He currently resides in San Jose CALIF and works for Santa-Clara Valley Transportation Authority as a bus operator.

This book is dedicated to both my birth-mother who gave me up for adoption but left me with three things: a pencil, a pad of paper and my imagination and my adoptive mother who did not give me life but made me a life and for believing in me when I did not believe in myself.......
thank you both!